The
Peacock
Feather

The twins have been successful in taking the reader through a labyrinth of expression so that the reader can imagine the events described in these short stories. The writing is brilliant, engaging and each story has its own uniqueness.

R.K. Anand, senior advocate and former Member of Parliament

The Kapoor brothers have communicated their inner truth brilliantly on the diverse aspects of life, emotion and love. From the book, one can infer the candidness of authors' journey of life and to pen down such thoughts in an alien language is a tribute to their personal genius.

Bhupinder Singh, former Chairman, State Trading Corporation

These short stories are quite engrossing, well worded and perfectly compliment their storytelling skills, imagination covering a wide range of subjects.

Suresh Kumar Raheja, singer and developer

An imaginative style of storytelling by Sunil and Sudhir. The Peacock Feather has wonderful overtones of adolescent infatuation combined with an evolving sense of mature realization. This story is exciting and sensuous and has a nice bitter sweet ending.

Raman Sehgal, curator, Luxembourg

All stories have been written so well, filled with drama, colour and emotions, the best part being the details depicted in them...one can really visualize the characters, their traumatic experiences and challenges faced by them.

Simran Bhargav, journalist and author

The
Peacock
Feather

Sunil Kapoor
& Sudhir Kapoor

RUPA

Published by
Rupa Publications India Pvt. Ltd 2017
7/16, Ansari Road, Daryaganj
New Delhi 110002

Sales centres:
Allahabad Bengaluru Chennai
Hyderabad Jaipur Kathmandu
Kolkata Mumbai

First published in Hardback 2017

ISBN: 978-81-291-4756-1

First impression 2017

10 9 8 7 6 5 4 3 2 1

Printed and bound in India by Repro Knowledgecast Limited, Thane

Contents

Preface

We were born as monozygotic twins. Science is yet to prove the telepathic connection between twins, but the anecdotal evidence is fascinating. Monozygotic twins are 100 per cent genetically matched and thus, we have similar personalities, thinking and intuitions. The twin factor unleashed a series of Comedy-of-Errors-like events in the years to come that began with our advent in this world.

Incidents took place one after another, which created confusion and complexities on account of being identical twins. The comical errors continued unabated during our stint at Modern School when the Maths teacher inadvertently punished one of the twins for the fault committed by the other. There were many incidences which led to hilarity. One close friend advised us to pen them down. This idea resulted in our writing 'The Terrible Twins'.

While writing the same we realized that in our interaction and working as chartered accountants and lawyers, we have met many people (either clients or government authorities or friends) from all walks of life, and each one of them had a different or unique story to tell. That, primarily, formed the genesis of this book.

Our house at Mall Road, Mussoorie, with a scintillating view of the Himalayan Range and our house at Dona Paula, Panjim, Goa with its breath-taking view of the Arabian Sea came in handy in writing these short stories.

A chance visit to Penang, Malaysia and Singapore where our daughter and son-in-law—Aanchal and Paarth Mehta—are staying, and the trials and tribulations faced by our sons—Anubhav & Ishaan Kapoor—in running restaurants formed the basis of 'King Cobra'.

A visit to Barot, the beautiful Hill Station in Himachal Pradesh, and observing an old torn photograph of Col. Batty in a tea stall, became the theme of 'An Accomplisher'.

A sojourn in the picturesque Kashmir valley and meeting with an old lady who had been a victim of partition, paved the way for writing 'Train to Wagah'. We had heard about the tragic incidences revealed by our father about the mayhem unleashed during the partition days, when he was one of the thousands of refugees from across the border who escaped a certain death and whose survival was not less than a miracle.

We decided to take a cue from these real life incidences and wrote these stories blending them, with some fictional and imaginary happenings to introduce some twist, turns and morals in them.

Whatever caps we may have donned during our journey of life, one thing that stands out the most is the hard work done with unflinching zeal in all the fields. We have observed that Life is like a book. Some chapters of it may be sad, some replete with excitement and happiness, but one thing is for sure, if you do not turn the page you shall never know what the next chapter has in store for you.

We would like to dedicate this book to our parents, Mr Shanker Kapoor and Mrs Rajni Kapoor, for their eternal support and belief in us.

SUNIL KAPOOR and SUDHIR KAPOOR
18 December 2016

The Peacock Feather

The sun was beginning to descend. A spectacular ball of crimson-orange—just a few minutes away from its magical dip into the horizon—on the far end of the Arabian Sea. The shimmering soft waves of water shone a deep pink as they were met by the River Mandovi that flows smoothly out from the Goan inland to merge with the sea. The view was breathtaking!

I watched that beautiful scene from the top-floor balcony of my house—a multistoried building called Bay View Heights located on a hill at Dona Paula. As my eyes swept over the valley below that leads to Caranzalem Beach and onwards to Miramar Beach at Panjim, the capital of Goa, I felt an immense peace with nature.

But just as suddenly that calm was replaced by an uncanny feeling. It felt as though the darkening clouds above and the green valley below heralded some special event—that the sun was setting as it did every day but the evening was going to be different. Many a time such thoughts creep into one's mind but they are obliterated as nothing untoward happens and one tends to forget them as quickly as they come. But there was something inexplicable in that moment that baffled me.

My wife Shivani—a strong-willed, intelligent lady, who could be very charming when she wanted—had earlier in the day mentioned a probable visit of an old friend of hers. The friend's name, Mohini, had struck me like a high-voltage current, opening up a secret vault to my first love and flashing memories of my youth across my mind. I had never disclosed that part of my life to anyone, not even to my wife. I had moved away from that memory till that afternoon when suddenly my heart had questioned my mind—could it be the same Mohini?

I stood on the balcony wondering what that strange feeling was. It made me restless. As I looked for an answer, the sun went down beyond the waters and the doorbell rang.

Her beautiful face looked back at me with the same innocence, that same smile. Yes, I recognized her immediately. She was *my* Mohini! In an instant, a reel of images ran across my dizzy head, engulfing my mind—the carefree days of my life in the 1970s, those blissful years of adolescence and teenage flashed before me. It had been a time of freedom with no stress, no responsibility and no worry. I had been so confident of conquering the world! It is another matter that what had then seemed so easy to accomplish, that ambition had slowly diminished over the years. I achieved about as much as any average person could—served a bank as a manager and then retired to an uneventful life in Goa. Goa, the heavenly abode for people seeking solitude and peace away from the madness of urban life...and a place of beautiful sunsets.

My thoughts were suddenly yanked back to reality as Mohini introduced herself as my wife's friend. It seemed that she had no recollection of me. I quickly stepped aside, allowing her to enter, wondering if she had caught my bewildered expression. Just then my wife came running from the bedroom. Amid laughter and excitement they met each other warmly. Shivani took her in and the two of them began exchanging notes right away as great friends do when they meet after a long interval.

I was left with my thoughts and they were completely jumbled up. Did my face ring a bell? Could she have placed me? No, it did not seem so. And, besides, how could she have, given the fact that I had never approached her all those years ago? What was I hoping for? Or maybe I had changed to the extent that she did not recognize me? Heavens! Had it been that long back that I left school? How difficult it is when one loves another intensely but that other has no inkling of it!

I went into my bedroom to freshen up before dinner. The sound of their laughter came through the closed door and it was with difficulty that I contained my thoughts. What a turn of events! The girl whom I had held as the pivot of my life at one time was sitting in my house today, and I was supposed to behave normally! Despite the years gone by, how on earth could I be expected to behave normally?

I put on a fresh shirt, dabbed on my favourite cologne and, taking a last look in the mirror, I returned to the living room. My head still spinning, I tried to join in their fun and, in an attempt at being jovial, gently reminded my wife that she had forgotten to introduce her friend to her husband. For a moment they stopped laughing and then burst out again. My wife, greatly amused, conducted the formality. The next quarter of an hour passed as they filled me in on their friendship. The two were classmates at Miranda House in Delhi University. They had studied English Literature at the University and had become good friends. Mohini's stint at Miranda was cut short because her parents relocated to Pune and she had completed her studies there. Over the years, the two had barely met but they remained in touch with each other through letters and email. Mohini married a businessman from Mumbai and lived there. Shivani told Mohini about her life, how she had adjusted her life according to my work postings from Lucknow to Gujarat to New Delhi and now Goa. But throughout these years they kept in touch. So when Mohini heard that she was to visit Goa to attend a seminar, the two ladies had been thrilled at the opportunity of meeting each other.

I listened to them in silence. There was a lot that I wanted to say, especially about Mohini and how I knew about her leaving Miranda House, but how could I speak? My mind was distracted. With the pretext of watching the evening news, I excused myself and moved to the television corner. As the evening entertainment blared from the TV set, I let my mind wander to that phase of my youth...the days when, for the first time, I set my eyes on that beautiful girl in the hill town of Mussoorie.

Mussoorie

Famously known as the 'Queen of Hills', Mussoorie, like the other hill stations of India, came into existence during the British Raj when the families of British colonials would shift to the hills to escape the scorching summer heat of the plains. Mussoorie derives its name from the Mansoor shrub (Coriaria nepalensis) that grows on those hills amid the sheer spread of pine and deodar trees. From Landour, one gets a panoramic view of a number of peaks of the majestic Himalayan mountain range—Nag Tibba, Yamunotri, Kedarnath, Badrinath and Nanda Devi, to name a few.

For ten years, I was a student at the renowned Doon School in Dehradun, a town situated near the base of the Mussoorie hills. As was the custom, the school organized periodic trips to the hills. In the morning students were taken by the school bus and dropped off at Kulri Mall Road in Mussoorie, with the standard strict instruction to return to the same spot by 4 p.m. for their return journey to school. We were told that any delay on our part would be reported to Mr Miller, the principal, and that defaulters would be punished. Those were days when we had limited pocket money and we spent every paisa in the most frugal manner possible. We also made the most of those visits to Mussoorie, doing as much as we could pack in.

During my final year in school, a favourite haunt of most students was Picture Palace, the first motion picture theatre in Mussoorie. For a long time, it ran the popular Hindi film *Sholay* and our school boys just could not get enough of it. Neither could I. It was a proud feat among the boys to attain the highest count of the number of times one had watched that popular movie. Mr Arthur Fisher was the manager at the theatre. Even now I can picture him—a tall man who was known to me because he knew my uncle who lived in Mussoorie. It was something to boast about.

During one such school visit, some boys rushed to the

roller skating rink even as many others scrambled for Picture Palace to catch the noon show. Along with a group of friends, I decided to go up to Gun Hill for its view. Gun Hill, at about 6000 feet, is the second highest point in Mussoorie (Lal Tibba in Landour, at 7500 feet, being the highest). It offers an impressive view of the beautiful Himalayan peaks as well as Doon Valley. Interestingly, during pre-independence days, a canon was fired from the top of the hill at midday to inform the local people of the time so that they could adjust their watches. Hence, the name. It is also known as Tope Tibba locally.

On the way to Gun Hill, as we passed Jhula Ghar—Mussoorie's adaptation of a neighbourhood amusement park—our attention was drawn towards screams and shouts of a group of girls on the giant wheel. In seconds my eyes fell on her. She was striking—fair with large eyes, red cheeks and long black hair that fell all over her excited face. I could not stop staring at the girl. All I remember is that I could not move. I stood transfixed. To add to it, an outdoor restaurant played a song from the romantic blockbuster *Bobby*. Classic Hindi-movie style! Was it love at first sight? I am not sure, but I was thrown off balance, especially during the impressionable teen age when falling in love is very easy.

The sight of her struck a deep chord in my heart. No girl had ever caught my attention like that before. I paid no heed to the calls of my friends and told them to move ahead, saying that I would join them later. If only the world would leave me alone so I could have my fill of her!

I spent one full rupee on a bottle of soda for the chance to continue standing there and looking her way. After her ride, she stepped down from the giant wheel and waited for her friends to do the same. She wore the uniform of Mussoorie International School and from what I could gather, she was in class nine or ten—about two or three years younger than I was. She passed me on her way out of the park, completely oblivious of my presence and continued walking towards the library end of town with her friends. I wanted to go after her but by then my friends had begun yelling and waving at me frantically from a distance. Reluctantly, I joined them.

On our way down, I looked out for her but could not locate her in the swarming crowd. I returned to Doon a miserable soul. School was never the same again. I found myself consistently engrossed in thoughts of her. I began to lack focus, to the exasperation of my teachers. It was the final year of my school life and I was not paying any attention to my studies. I could barely wait for another visit but, as luck would have it, none were scheduled. Three months passed by, and with each passing day I became more desperate to see her again. Unable to control myself any longer, I sneaked out of the school premises one Sunday morning and took a bus for Mussoorie from Rajpur Road. In spite of the precarious situation I had put myself in, that journey remains one of my most and more memorable ones. I had traversed the terrain innumerable times, yet on that occasion it seemed to come alive for the first time. I found myself humming happily till I reached Mussoorie and was the first to alight from the bus. I ran towards Jhula Ghar, totally unmindful of the surging crowds. I spotted some girls in the girl's school uniforms, but could not find her. I ran back towards Mall Road and there she was, viewing Doon Valley through a set of binoculars positioned in front of Chic Chocolate Shop and Cottage Industry Emporium. She stood there with her friends. When I went closer and I heard one of her friends call out her name—Mohini. How apt! Certainly, she was beautiful.

The group made its way to lunch. I followed them to a restaurant called Neelam, wondering why they could not have chosen Kwality that served a better food. They hurriedly had their food, talking and chuckling constantly, and made a quick exit after paying up. I watched as they crossed the road to Inder's Sweet Shop, it being the usual practice for diners from Neelam to stop by for Inder's famous chocolate barfis. Then the girls were on the road, running in the direction of their school. In minutes it was all over. I sat back staring at my sandwich. Since it had served its purpose, I was no longer hungry. I had it packed. Boarders did not waste food. I went out into the afternoon sunshine, so glad for the chance of having seen her again. That was my second encounter. I recall noticing that she seemed taller than the first time I saw her. She was now almost my height, and she looked even more beautiful than before.

After I came back and entered the premises of my school, I was hauled up. Not only was I severely reprimanded by Mr Miller but I was also given an ultimatum—that if I ever dared to repeat what I had done, I would be sent off marching from school. Bunking in a boarding school and that too from a prestigious institution such as Doon School was considered a serious offence, at least if one was caught.

In the remaining months of that final year, on the occasions we were allowed a night out, I managed a couple of visits to Mussoorie through my local guardian. Once in town, I would wait for the Mussoorie International girls to appear on Mall Road. She never disappointed. Whether she was having food at a restaurant or skating at the rink or simply sauntering around, I followed her everywhere she went. Just seeing her was bliss. However, whenever I tried to get myself to go up and speak to her, I failed miserably. Leave alone the guts, I totally lacked the confidence for such a venture. I hated myself for it. There were moments when I would find her alone, yet I let even those chances go by. I knew I was being an idiot.

One particular visit often comes to mind when I think about those days. It was the most difficult of all my escapades. I followed Mohini and her friends to Landour, a small cantonment town next to Mussoorie. It is a steep climb from Mussoorie's Mall Road to Landour. To avoid being seen, at every turn of the hill, I had to run for cover behind foliage. I would have made a hilarious sight if anyone had seen me. I had no idea where they were headed until they arrived at The Parsonage, the house of Victor Banerjee, a famous actor. The girls were very excited to see him on the verandah, and what turned out to be a bonus was that Tom Altar, another well-known actor, and the famous writer, Ruskin Bond, were with him, sharing a pot of tea. I was pleasantly surprised too. They obliged by giving their autographs to the girls.

On the way back, Mohini and her friends took the route via Wynberg Allen School since one of them studied there, and then the rest made their way to Mussoorie International. I, of course, continued in the same manner, trying my best not to get noticed. That was my last visit to those hills during school life. I was by then completely obsessed with her. Life had no meaning otherwise. I do not know how I managed my emotions, or how I completed those last months of school. Her glowing face remained etched in my mind and her infectious laugh continued to haunt me. And all the time I had not made myself known to her, only because I had lacked courage.

School life came to an end. With my Senior Cambridge examinations, the Mussoorie chapter of my life was over. Thereafter, I joined Hindu College in Delhi University to pursue a course in commerce. Of course, I did visit the hill town several times afterwards, but things were not the same.

I came back to reality with a deep breath and switched channels; I had barely watched the news. I looked towards the ladies chatting away merrily. They were busy and dinner was still being readied, so I nestled back in the couch and continued with my thoughts, quietly enjoying the tête-à-tête with myself.

Delhi

College time was enjoyable and I soon got into the rhythm of life in Delhi. But I missed Mohini. I found my thoughts frequently straying towards her. And then it happened one evening during the Hindu festival of Janmashtami. I was at the Jhandewalan Temple when I thought I saw her in the distance. My heart raced and I quickly threaded my way through the crowds to manage a better view. Yes, it was her. She appeared to be with her younger sister. I was desperate to know about her whereabouts and what she was doing; but since trying to follow her through the large gathering of people seemed a pointless attempt, I waited at the entrance gate. It seemed a smart thing to do at that time, for when they were leaving, I was able to note down the number of their carrow dust coloured Ambassador car. At least it was something! The incident encouraged me. It gave me hope that she too was in Delhi and now there was a chance to meet and express my feelings to her.

In the coming months, I chanced to meet her, or rather see her several times. The first of these was during a visit to the Chanakya film theatre with my family. I spotted her parked car. We were scheduled to watch the evening show and were running late, but I was not going to miss that chance of seeing her. So I stayed out on some pretext and promised my family I would join them as soon as possible. It paid off. I remained within view of her car and was close enough to hear her voice as she came to the parking area with her mother. They had watched the earlier show, and as they got into the car they instructed the driver to take them to Miranda House. That information was all I needed. She was studying in Delhi University and that too in North Campus, just like I was. I could not have been luckier!

By the time I took my seat inside the hall, I had missed the beginning. My family was astonished. I had done the unthinkable—the film being my all-time favourite actor Amitabh Bachhan's *Amar Akbar Anthony*. Not that it made any difference. My mind remained elsewhere for most part of the rest of the movie anyway.

What followed was quite predictable. It did not take me long to locate her at Miranda House. Soon I had identified her favourite places of visit—the shops, university canteens, Deepaul's at Janpath, Bengali Market and British Council Library. Once, she left her handkerchief on a table at a restaurant in

Bengali Market. I picked it up. It felt strange to hold something that had been so close to her. It remained with me for a long time and though I have since lost it, the perfume that it held still lingers in my mind.

Weeks passed. I was happy again and looked forward to the times I could see her. Coincidentally, my uncle was in charge at the British Council Library on the street called Rafi Marg in those days. I began making regular visits there, especially on Saturdays when she mostly visited the library. On that particular Saturday, as I browsed the fiction section, I finally saw her at the counter. Having placed her books on a table, Mohini was busy filling a form. Seizing the opportunity, I quietly inserted a bookmark with a note into one of her volumes. It was a peacock feather. My writing on the note read: 'A lucky charm from an admirer.' It is believed that a peacock feather is a symbol of good luck and well-being. It was my lucky charm and I wanted her to have it.

She completed the form and, taking no notice of my action, went out. The next Saturday I waited for her but she did not come to the library. There was no sign of her in the coming weeks either. Unfortunately, that was the last I was to see of her as she left college all of a sudden. I made enquiries but could not find any information. There was no way of locating her. For the second time my love story came to a halt. I was heartbroken. I found myself at the same crossroads and cursed myself for not having made my move earlier. Why did I wait so long? I had only myself to blame. A time of brooding followed. I became a recluse. Days passed and I immersed myself in books. At the end of the year, I cleared my final examinations and eventually joined a nationalized bank, posted in Lucknow.

Back to Goa

My flashback was interrupted by my wife telling me that dinner was served. I was curious to know more about Mohini. How had life been for her? Was she happy? I joined them at the dining table but could not make myself look at her. I must have remained quiet for a while, for Mohini, taking one look in my direction, remarked that her husband too did not speak much.

Silly woman, I thought. Here I was bursting to say so much. If only I could tell her that. I smiled and muttered something. It was amazing how the distance between us as we sat across the table assumed a different measure mentally. She was absolutely unaware of what I felt for her.

The next three days were the best days of my life. Mohini was staying with her colleagues at Marriott Hotel—located near Dona Paula in North Goa—which was close to our place. Once she was done with her official commitments, she would spend all her time with us. My wife was surprised at my level of involvement with her friend. I had never engaged in the same manner with any of her friends earlier. If she felt offended she never expressed it. However, she did remark that she could sense a change in her husband. Why else would he, suddenly, be spending his hard-earned savings on trimmings for the home, not to mention the flowers, the chocolates and air-fresheners? Those were my words thrown back at me, for I was always reminding her to be careful with wasteful expenses.

I needed to be careful, I told myself. Was I overdoing it? All I wanted was for Mohini to have a good time and she seemed to be doing so and that too in my company. What more could I ask for? I was a happy man.

One of my friends had once mentioned that it was strange but true that one's first love returned back to one's life in one way or the other.

Mohini had emerged from nowhere and had spent almost three days sitting next to me. So close yet so far.

I acquainted her with interesting bits of information about Goa, beginning with the name itself—how Goa originated from the word 'gai', meaning cow in Hindi. 'Many years ago, when Sage Parshuram visited the area, he came with his cows. He prayed and gave the name of Goa to the virgin lands lying alongside the Arabian Sea.' Then there is the tale of Lover's Point in Dona Paula. It is filled with pathos, and first-time visitors find it fascinating. Mohini did too. 'Dona Paula was the name of a Portuguese governor's daughter. According to history, she fell in love with a poor fisherman. Her father was against their alliance, so the lovers jumped into the sea to end their lives together. The spot from where they jumped is called Lover's Point.' I had never enjoyed sightseeing so much. We visited the beaches Goa is famous for: Calangute and Candolim in the north and Valsova and Colva in the south. And from delightful food at the shacks at Baga Beach to ice creams at Miramar, we covered it all in those three days. Everything was perfect. I even sang for her, to my own surprise. Goa is known to be an enchanting place and Mohini loved it.

It was time for her to leave. On that day, according to

plan, the Marriott shuttle was to take Mohini and her group to Dabolim airport in the afternoon. My heart was heavy, yet I was grateful for having seen her again. Nothing could compare with that. And I was glad that by chance my daughters were arriving that same evening. My mind, I hoped, would be diverted from thoughts of her.

As it is known to happen before a person's departure, there is a last-minute scramble for unfinished work. Our morning shopping, too, took us more time than we had anticipated. By the time we arrived at the Marriott, the shuttle had left for the airport, much to Mohini's embarrassment. Shivani suggested I drop her off since I was to make the trip to the airport in any case, while she oversaw the dinner and other arrangements for the arrival of our daughters.

Life seemed to be throwing a lot of surprises my way. Driving to the airport with Mohini seated next to me was a dream come true and during the forty minutes that it took us, I found myself speaking without a pause. Any silence would have been awkward. I mentioned the tourist spots we had not covered and that could be seen on her next visit, the festivals of Goa, the laid-back life of the Goan people and so on. Mohini spoke very little; I barely gave her a chance.

As we walked towards the departure gate at the airport, still exchanging the mundane, something snapped within me. Suddenly, I took stock of the situation. Was I going to let the moment pass? Would I ever get the chance again? No! 'Now,' I told myself. 'Now is the time!' My heart began to pound. I turned towards her before any conflicting thought in my head could stop me, and told her that I had something to say to her.

It was about the past. I looked at her face. She looked back at me, and then she began to smile—a mischievous yet warm smile slowly spread over her beautiful face. She looked the same sweet girl I had fallen madly in love with thirty years ago.

She asked me what it was that I wished to say. But before I could answer, she asked me if I wanted to talk about my following her in Mussoorie? Bengali Market? Or, maybe, Miranda House and British Council Library? Wasn't I watching her and her friends from distance when they were with Victor Banerjee, Tom Alter and Ruskin Bond at the Personage? I stood rooted, completely stumped. How could I have been so stupid? She had known all along! The handkerchief, the conversations to help me find her... had all been deliberate clues! If only I had picked on them! Did I remember the peacock feather, she asked. Of course I did! How could I forget that precious symbol of my feelings for her. 'I still have it,' she said gently. She blurted in the same breath 'Do you still possess the handkerchief which I had purposely left at the restaurant for you. From the corner of my eye I saw you picking that up.' I didn't have the heart to reply in the negative and responded in the affirmative. 'Well, she blurted, I was keen to meet you and at times my eyes searched for you.'

I was numb. I had nothing more to say. I did not have to. Mohini gave me the most endearing smile and then she turned and walked into the airport lounge. I stood there staring after her for a long time.

It was a bitter sweet end to my love story and maybe it was the Peacock Feather which had brought her back in my life even so for a short while.

The Gutka King

A cavalcade of seven cars from Mumbai made its way into the small town of Madhopur in Maharashtra in the twilight hours of morning. Four white sedans, including two BMW 7 Series and two Mercedes-Benz S-Class, carried the family of the Seth, and another two smart black SUVs, one each at the front and rear ends, carried the security staff. These made up six of the impressive line-up of vehicles. The Seth himself was seated in his white Rolls Royce that bore his name embossed in pure gold: Roshan Lal Maheshwari.

As news of the arrival spread, it grew louder and the fleet wounding through the by-lanes stopped in front of the grey and white building of the town hall. All the cars carried presents for the people of the town who were eagerly awaiting the arrival of the Seth or, as he was popularly known, Gutka King.

The sarpanch garlanded Seth Roshan Lal as he warmly welcomed him and his family. They were his guests whom he had specially invited for the Independence Day celebrations to be held the next morning. The seth gave generous donations to the panchayat for the construction of a hospital and a school building in town, and the family distributed the presents they had brought from Mumbai. Then they proceeded into the hall for the elaborate feast that had been prepared in his honour. Afterwards, Seth Roshan Lal and his son spent an hour with the sarpanch and other senior members of the town to discuss further developmental projects for which the Seth's sanction was required. Arrangements for their stay had been made at the dak bungalow, that being the best available accommodation in the town.

Seth Roshan Lal was an early riser. He woke up at 5.00 a.m. the next day when it was still dark and walked alone towards the river Gehar. It is called 'gehar', meaning deep in the native language, perhaps because the depth of the river is immeasurable at certain points. He climbed a large boulder on the riverbank and, looking across towards the dense forest on the other side, fixed his eyes on the foreboding wilderness beyond.

He was tall in his trademark white attire, lean and upright. As he stood facing the breeze, a lock of white hair flew, softening the sharp features on his face while also revealing the determined hard lines that defined the story of his life. From his appearance no one could tell his age. He stood strong and in good shape for his seventy-nine years.

The first ray of the rising sun began to light up the woods in the distance. The year was 2009 and as he continued to gaze across the river, something churned deep down in his heart. He went into a reverie, remembering his childhood days and how his journey had begun from the forest that changed his life forever. Seth went down the memory lane and reminisced about his state of affairs-seventy five long years back.

✓

The year was 1934. The dark brown eyes of four-year-old Roshan strained to see as far as they could as he stood on his toes for a better view. He could make out the far bend on the road outside the forest from where, any minute now, his father would enter the small path leading to their hut. He wanted to be the first to spot him.

The Maheshwari family lived on the outskirts of Ranthambore in present-day Rajasthan. Their abode, a small square mud hut, measured barely ten feet on one side, but it was there that the six children—three brothers and three sisters—dwelt with their father and mother. The family lived in fear, dreading the day the forest officers would demolish their small home, their single source of stability. They were the poorest of the poor and lived life one day at a time. Each morning they woke up with one wish for the day—that at the end of it they would sleep with food in their stomachs.

In that remote area of Ranthambore there were no schools and playgrounds for children, not even shops. Nothing at all! Only a thick forest that was a natural habitat of wild animals such as the leopards, jungle cats, wild boars and blue bulls; and from where the occasional calls of langur monkeys could be heard alerting the other creatures when they saw the majestic Royal Bengal Tiger appear. The deer, including the sambar and the spotted chital, were alert at all times and fled the moment predators moved from the river bank towards their part of the deep forest.

It was almost dark. A sheet of fireflies shone over the

vegetation around the hut while the jackals howled, but Roshan's father Ghanshyam was not yet home. Roshan's mother, Sitara Devi, looked at him anxiously. Though the youngest of her children, Roshan was the most forceful of the lot, always demanding and questioning. Many a time he displayed courage by venturing alone into the deep forest to gather broken branches without any fear. And even at that young age, his ability to observe and question the rationale behind the pitiable condition of the family was baffling.

Roshan saw the tall figure of his father almost running towards them. All the children had been waiting, staring in the same direction for some time now, but it was Roshan who yelled out first. Their father's hands waving to them from the distance was a signal for them to hurry with their assigned duties. He had brought provisions with him. There would be food tonight! They swung into action. As Sitara Devi and her oldest daughter Rukmani prepared for the cooking in a clearing beside the hut, the others brought the necessary material to support them. Ram, the eldest of all the children, ran for the pail of clean water he had filled from the river that flowed nearby, having braved the possible appearance of an animal or even a cobra or krait on the way. Mohan had firewood neatly stacked and he fetched the bundle immediately, while Roshan went inside the hut to fetch the eight bowls the family had. He had cleaned them in readiness for the hopeful evening meal to be served in.

Sitara Devi and Rukmani cooked lentils and chapatis made of bajra, all the while shouting instructions to the two younger girls, Renu and Khushi, who rather than helping them, kept getting in the way of progress as they skipped about excitedly. Once readied, the food was hurriedly served and each member made a grab for a bowl. They ate in silence and in haste, barely chewing, for they could not wait. Every morsel was consumed and the cool river water was downed to fill any space left in the stomach. Once done, they sat back and looked at each other, satisfaction shone in their eyes. It was a lot to be grateful for. The boys then slept around the burnt-out fire where they had eaten, while the parents and the girls slept inside the hut. On the days the father returned home with provisions, such was the norm.

Every morning, Ghanshyam walked to the small village near Ranthambore to find work. If he were lucky, he did various tasks: from carrying tourists' baggage, to sweeping the floors of the ancient temple, to pulling carts when the trucks brought bricks from a kiln factory forty kilometres away. He did petty jobs and earned about four to five rupees as daily wages. On the days he did not get any work, he would return home empty-handed, bracing himself for the suffering his family would endure. The children would see him walk home and from his demeanour realize instantly that they would have to sleep without eating. They would drink water to try and douse the fire burning in their bellies, hunger mirrored in their eyes. And as they lay beside each other, looking up at the stars shining in the night sky, they would curse their plight.

This went on for a few years. Roshan was ten years of age by the time Ghanshyam was able to save some money. Looking for better work opportunities, the family moved to Madhopur where a relative of theirs lived. Madhopur was a village then, but because of its cultivation of tobacco and beetle nut, there was economic progress. Ghanshyam set up a stationery shop in the local bazaar. He was still poor but was now able to feed his family. There were times when Ram would buy old books and magazines from the neighbouring town of Satara and sell them for a profit at their shop. The earning so made, though small, allowed them a third meal. It was no less than a celebration.

Ghanshyam was keen that the young Roshan join the local government school and begin his studies like his elder brothers. However, since Roshan had never attended school, starting now meant attending class with boys much younger to him, so he refused! His dignity would not accept such an insult. He was not born to be laughed at. Moreover, he had developed an aversion for the headmaster. On a visit to the school once to meet his brothers, Roshan had witnessed him caning some boys and had taken an immediate dislike towards him.

One day, as Roshan played with his friends in front of his house, a fakir came by asking for alms. He looked at Roshan's face and calling his mother to the door, told her that her child was going to shine in the years to come. Sitara Devi was happy and, taking his words as sacrosanct, she immediately brought a bowl of rice for him. Roshan thought it a ploy for extracting alms and rebuked his mother for being generous; but in his heart he was extremely pleased. He was a shrewd boy and aware that he was the one singled out for praise from amongst all the children present. He basked in the attention he got, but more than that he kept the words of the fakir in mind.

Ghanshyam began to get impatient with Roshan and insisted that he joined school. The father believed that the young fellow was wasting his time spending all his waking hours either playing with his friends or swimming in the Gehar River. But Roshan had other plans. He wanted to join his father and help him in the business. Ghanshyam reasoned with him—Ram had already begun assisting him at the shop, and if Roshan went to school, he would be educated and would grow in life. He could then work in a big city like Amravati. But big cities did not mean anything to Roshan. He had no knowledge of them; he had never visited any. His mere acquaintance with the 'big' life was the movement of the occasional cars, trucks and jeeps that passed through Madhopur. These were enough to help him understand the importance of machines. At that tender age he realized that without the massive support of technology in reducing human burden man could not make any progress.

He told his father defiantly that he was not going to waste his time on studies, and also that if his father did not allow him to sit at the shop, he would start his own business. Ghanshyam did not appreciate rebelliousness of that kind. He did not approve of Roshan's resentment to studies and, particularly, his stubbornness at that young age. He expected Roshan to fulfil the desires of his parents and expressed it so. Unknown to his father, Roshan was however not squandering his time. Perpetually restless and desperate to make use of his life, he had begun visiting the sole workshop in the village. He would stand there for hours, observing the mechanics, completely fascinated by the deftness of their hands and the workings of the machines. The workshop did not boast of any fancy equipment, but to Roshan it represented action. He had no technical knowledge of equipment; nonetheless, being a good observer, he soon learnt the basics.

Roshan was denied permission by his father to sit at the shop. It was a blow but the boy had a burning desire to do business, so he put his plans to action. He took stock of his entire savings—five rupees—it was all that the eleven-year-old had to begin his business with. He bought two bottles of blue ink, positioned himself at the gates of Mohan's school and began to sell loose ink at a profit. Examinations were on and many a time, in the midst of writing a paper, students needed to refill their pens. They would run to Roshan. Soon, his ink became famous. It was a novel idea; nobody had ever thought of doing such a thing. Although Mohan did not approve of it as everyone knew Roshan was his younger brother, the latter paid no heed. His mind was filled with innovative ideas and he was determined to put them to good use. Roshan was sharp. He thought of ways to provide facilities to students so he could earn money. He knew what the key requirements for a business were in order to be successful—one needed to be a pioneer in any work and give people what they needed; and at their doorsteps, if possible. And he was smart enough to design new ways to reach out to his customers. He sold loose sheets of paper, exercise books, foot rulers, erasers, paper clips and other stationery items. He also learnt to mend faulty pens. And all of this was done without owning a shop or renting one, paying taxes or issuing receipts to customers. In a year's time he had a business that ran almost parallel to that of his father. No longer were students required to go to the market; they purchased what they wanted right outside the school. Roshan added further value. He also began a system of taking orders for stationery. Students could place requests at school and he would deliver at their homes. Further, he purchased a bicycle to carry a couple of children to and from school.

Roshan still had the mornings free, so he started distributing Marathi and Hindi newspapers. He would go to the railway station at 5.00 a.m. for his supply of the day's papers, and then deliver these to the respective addresses in the village on his bicycle. It was not long before Roshan won the hearts of his village people. He was helpful and he earned the reputation of dependability—he completed any task given to him. He also exemplified a strength of character that most others of his age fell short of. There was a time when he jumped into the Gehar, in spite of the strong current, to save an old man belonging to another village whose boat had capsized. Incidents such as these endeared him to his people.

Six years passed in Madhopur and Roshan grew to be a tall and tough seventeen-year-old. His years of hard labour and struggle lent him a lean and muscular build. He looked older than his peers and was more mature than them too. By then, he was the owner of a small but successful business.

Now Roshan always had a penchant for adventure. Any opportunity for indulging in an exciting activity had his fullest participation. The one thing he and his friends had not yet done was cross the Gehar that skirted the village. The dense forest that lay on the other side was home to tigers, leopards, wild hogs, hyenas and snakes. The children of the village were not allowed to cross over. It was absolutely forbidden. But Roshan would stand at the edge of the river and know in his heart that one day he would visit the forest when the time came. And it did. The day dawned when he and two of his friends, Chander Dutt and Ramesh Lal, decided it must be done. That late afternoon they swam across Gehar. The current was slow and the water cool and, effortlessly, they entered the forest on the other side.

The boys explored their surroundings, enjoying the thrill of venturing beyond the limits of their daily lives. Bending forward to pick a stray betel nut from the ground, Chander almost fell over on the shrill call of a monkey, sending the others laughing. They huddled closer as they slowly ventured deeper into the denseness of tree cover. Then they heard the first shouts. It was a mix of screaming and hollering. Startled, they crouched together and hid behind trees fearing should they be seen. Madhopur was a small village and any misconduct or out-of-decorum behaviour was instantly reported back to the elders. In their case, severe punishment was guaranteed for the rule they had broken. The sound of voices was faint at first and then it became louder. Suddenly, all hell broke loose. A gun shot sounded and there was heavy running in their direction. There was only one way to go—deeper into the forest! Clutching each other they ran, not sure of where or from what. The shouts of people seemed to be at their heels.

Chander screamed there were people after them. What they could not have guessed was that they were poachers! The boys did not know what poaching meant. They had no idea that animals were killed for their body parts and skins and that, though it was considered a criminal offence, there was a market for it. Only when they heard a loud thud, followed by the ear-splitting trumpet of an elephant and one more gun shot, did they realize that something else was happening. Curious to know what it was, they turned around and ran back to the scene of action. Now they saw the enormous pit that had been dug in the ground to catch the elephants; they had not noticed it earlier. Elephants were a rarity in that forest. The poachers had spotted the tusker and his companion and planned the trap—it was an opportunity they did not want to miss. The animals had not seen the danger, the pit having been camouflaged with plants. The tusker fell in and was shot dead. The poachers were now targeting a female elephant who was wounded and was running berserk.

When the trio, oblivious of the danger they were heading into, saw the pit they were dazed. They tried to gain control of the situation but it was too late. The injured elephant charged in their direction. They ran, but had barely covered a short distance before Chander was shot at the back of his head by a poacher's bullet. He was dead before he hit the ground. What followed was total mayhem. The poachers, overtaken by greed, were not going to let go of their catch. They chased the elephant and fired furiously, shouting instructions at each other. And on the trees the monkeys shrieked at the top of their voices, perhaps signalling a warning to each other of the biggest predators on the ground—the poachers!

Roshan stopped in his tracks, devastated. He looked at the lifeless Chander, not sure what to do. Then, realizing that they needed to save their own lives, he started running again, calling out to Ramesh to do the same. But Ramesh remained in a trance, staring down at Chander's body, unable to move.

Before Roshan could reach out and help his friend, the female elephant charged over Ramesh, almost crushing him right there. There was nothing left for Roshan but to make his escape. He ran with all his strength, with no sense of direction. Farther and farther into the forest he went. He had to get away. After what seemed an eternity, the sound of the elephant faded away. Believing he was safe, he slowed down. A bullet whizzed past! The poachers were now after *him* because he had witnessed their crime. They could not let him get away so easily. Roshan was exhausted. He could not run anymore. Frantically, he looked for somewhere to hide. Luckily, he stumbled upon a gap in the undergrowth. It was a small cave-like hole formed by the slanting trunk of a fallen tree, half-hidden behind a thick growth of thorny bushes. He crouched into it, grateful for the chance to recover, his aching legs buckling under him. But to his shock, he discovered he was not alone. In the fading light he found himself staring at the outline of an eleven-foot python. What a nightmare! The reptile eyed him. Roshan waited, his heart in his mouth, his life hanging in thin air, wondering which of the two to save himself from—the creature in front of him or those he was running away from. But the reptile did not move. Having devoured a whole deer, it was immobile— at least for the moment.

The voices of the poachers became clear as they approached closer. They looked about but, mercifully, did not notice the hole in the vegetation and decided not to waste any more time. Dusk was fast approaching and they wanted to get back to their kill. They had a rich haul to take care of. The ivory of the tusker—or white gold as it was called—would fetch them a fortune. They left, saying the boy could not possibly survive in the heart of the jungle once night had fallen. What happened thereafter, no matter much he tried to recall in later years, Roshan could not logically put together as a cohesive whole. It remains in fragments till today. All he is sure of, as the voices of the departing poachers faded away, was his immediate need to get himself out of that space in the undergrowth. He could not bear to have his companion eye him a second more. He stumbled out, the way he had gone in, feeling his way around the tree trunk with his hands, the bush thorns biting into his flesh.

He remembered how it was almost dark, and that in the light of the waning moon rising in the sky he could just about make out the shapes in the forest. The fear he felt in his heart remains unforgettable. All he wanted was to run, to keep moving, to escape. But without Chander and Ramesh he could not return to the village. He must have run blindly for hours before he saw fire torches and heard loud voices coming his way. Were they the poachers again? Or, perhaps, people looking for him? He did not want to get caught.

∿

The year was 1948. Roshan sat on the steps of a temple, slowly eating the prasad the punditji had given him. He always spent some moments that way in the late afternoons before leaving the temple precincts. Suddenly, a clattering sound broke his thoughts. Looking up towards the temple shrine enclosure, he saw an old man in the midst of a seizure—the puja thali had dropped from his hands and was clattering down the steps. Roshan recognized him. He was a regular devotee who offered prayers every Monday. Roshan sprang to his feet and dashed up the stairs, managing to reach the old man just as the latter touched the ground. Roshan understood it was an emergency and, as there were very few people around during that time of day, he took charge of the situation. He ran for the old man's car parked outside the temple complex and then, along with the driver, he took the patient to the nearest hospital. The man was attended to in time and he survived.

The old man was Mallika Arjun Pillai, fondly referred to as Sethji—owner of the largest tobacco farms of Shimoga district in Mysore, in present-day Karnataka. He was extremely grateful to the boy. He acknowledged that if it were not for the timely assistance he received, he would not have lived. Once he resumed his regular duties, Mallika Arjun called for Roshan to express his gratitude with a monetary reward, but when he looked at the robust young fellow with the arresting eyes standing before him, he had another idea—that of employing him.

Mallika Arjun was seventy-two. He had never married and had no children of his own. On account of his age and heart ailment, he found it increasingly difficult to physically oversee his vast fields and farmlands. He had six hundred acres of farming area that lay on the outskirts of Shimoga district. A large portion of this land was earmarked for his tobacco crop, he being mainly a tobacco cultivator; but he also grew other cash crops—areca nut and betel leaf. The problem was his business had begun to go into losses. Sethji had been thinking of hiring an able hand—a field assistant who could be on his feet, coordinating and overseeing the activities of cultivation under the chief supervisor. When he met the boy, he instantly sensed a bright spark in his eyes—a spark he could trust. He offered him the work of an assistant supervisor. Though Roshan was young for the post, he looked the part, coming as he did from the soil. What was more, he had only just proved himself. To Mallika Arjun, he seemed most suited for the work. Roshan accepted the offer. He was overjoyed and thought it a miracle. He put his heart and soul into his work, and he slogged day and night to live up to the responsibility and trust that had been placed on his young shoulders. It was not long before he was able to identify the reasons for the business running in losses. Firstly, there was no control over the wild beasts that wandered into the cultivation area and spoiled the tobacco plants. Secondly, there was widespread pilferage wherein unscrupulous employees sold crop to their business competitors at compromised rates. Further, poachers moved about freely on the farmland without restriction. Then, there were large-scale thefts at the warehouse as well where tobacco was stored for the making of kimam—a dried paste of tobacco, spices and additives processed together—a popular product in the market.

Roshan realized that he would have to take up each challenge one at a time. It was not going to be easy, and he was sure to make many enemies in the process. But he was determined to get the business back on its feet. He thought carefully of his course of action and requested a meeting with Mallika Arjun whom he addressed, like everyone else, as Sethji. Roshan appraised Sethji of the state of affairs and sought his permission to eliminate the problems. The old man was shocked. The revelation came as a setback as he had never expected it. The people he had relied on had let him down. He had not been informed of anything other than the destruction caused by wild animals.

He decided to trust the boy for *he* had shown loyalty, and decided that he, himself, would face the consequences of it. Sethji gave his permission and instructed Roshan to ask for any assistance that he might require and, further, to spare no cost. He was given a free hand. In a matter of months, Roshan changed the entire scene of the business. As a first step he restricted the entry of animals. Wherever required and under his own supervision, he had the cultivation areas barricaded with fencing and he patrolled these areas day and night carrying Sethji's .303 rifle on his shoulder. His second step was to build his own team of trusted hands. He needed help in all areas of operation; it was not a job to be done alone. This inner core group remained continuously on its feet and worked in rotation till it had considerable control over the business functions. The chief supervisor did not dare object, for he was guilty.

In a matter of a few months, the change became apparent. The business did a complete turnaround and started making profits. Sethji was immensely proud, not only of Roshan's outstanding performance but also of his own judgement—he had been right. The young fellow was loyal, sincere and honest. He made an offer to Roshan—a 5 per cent share in his farms. At that time Roshan was just nineteen.

Years passed by. By the time Roshan turned twenty-five, he had taken considerable charge of Sethji's work. He was an excellent manager, tough and clever. Sethji, extremely pleased, increased his share from 5 per cent to 20 per cent. Roshan's hard work and unflinching zeal yielded rich dividends. He earned himself a strong foothold in the company and became Sethji's right hand, heading all his business operations.

Roshan had by this time saved a considerable amount of his income. He requested leave for a month. Sethji now kept unwell more than ever; he could no longer function without Roshan and relied heavily on his shoulders, yet he gave his consent. In all the years it was the first time Roshan had asked for a leave. The young man deserved it. Roshan bought presents of clothing and jewellery, borrowed Sethji's jeep and left for Madhopur—a distance of six hundred kilometres from Shimoga. He arrived at the village late at night. Nothing had changed except that the condition of the place had worsened. He stopped his vehicle in the main market area and looked about it, dismayed. He was not prepared for what he saw. He wondered how it was possible for a place to have stood still for so many years—nine long years—while his entire world had transformed. He felt a lump in his throat and tears began to roll down his cheeks as he drove up to his home.

The door stood ajar. Roshan stepped over the threshold holding his breath, not knowing what to expect. There was no one in the outer room but he could hear voices. He strode across and stood in the connecting doorway. They were in the inner room. A dim light threw shadows over the dismal condition of those present there. The same worn-out look that Roshan had seen on the outside seemed to have permeated his home's walls and had come to rest with his family. There was no furniture; his father and older brothers sat on a floor mat as food was served to them by two ladies Roshan did not recognize. There was no sight of his sisters. His mother sat in a corner of the room, bent over her meal. On seeing her, Roshan instinctively rushed forward, unable to contain himself any longer.

There were exclamations of shock—at first they thought someone had barged in, then realization dawned upon them. Indeed, it was Roshan! Tears and laughter mingled as the family tried to register that their Roshan was back. They began to exclaim and question. Where had he been all these years? The parents were overjoyed and, at first, so were Ram and Mohan. Then the brothers withdrew themselves with a look of displeasure on their faces. They told him of the rumour that had spread in the village after his disappearance. It was believed that the three of them, he, Chander and Ramesh had fled to the cities to look for better prospects—like other boys in the village had done before them. They had left their poor families behind with little regard for them. As the years passed, and since there was no news from them, it was taken that they had abandoned their village. Chander's father had died the previous year, waiting for his one and only son to return, while the parents of Ramesh, who were in an acute financial crisis, prayed for their son's return so he could put an end to their miseries.

Roshan's family had been heartbroken. They could not understand why after having worked so hard had he chosen to leave his business. Had he lacked the courage to share the slow progress of the family? Where had he gone? They were upset as he had not informed them of his whereabouts or asked after their wellbeing. Had something happened to him? Ghanshyam and Sitara Devi now looked at Roshan and became silent, but the brothers continued to give vent to their emotions. Roshan wanted to deny the allegations and tell them what had truly transpired—about the forbidden visit to the forest, the poachers, and the death of his friends. And thereafter he feared that if he returned he would be held responsible for their deaths. That he had decided it was best to escape, so he had crossed the forest to the other side in the midst of a group of hunters he had run into that night, and had further travelled to Mysore. How he had wandered aimlessly for two years, doing odd jobs to survive. He had missed his home the most during the declaration of India's independence in 1947, and had desperately wanted to be with his family, but fear had overruled his better sense. He had then come to the temple that was to be his home, his sanctuary. At first the pundit, whom he later addressed as punditji, had taken him in out of pity, but he soon developed a liking to the poor boy who was ready to clean the floors of the temple and do sundry work for food in return. And then Roshan met Mallika Arjun. But Roshan did not tell them all this. It was best to let things be, he thought, so he did not mention the forest. He told them of his work in Shimoga and how Sethji trusted him. He also added that in all the years he had been away, he had worked in honesty and done nothing his family would be ashamed of. The brothers embraced each other and the past years were put behind them. The fact was that Roshan had returned and, by the look of him and his expensive clothes, he seemed to have done well for himself. All was forgiven and forgotten when he gave them the presents he had brought for them.

His sisters, he was told, were married. Rukmani lived in Amravati while the younger two were in Satara. The two ladies at home he did not recognize were Ram and Mohan's wives.

Roshan wished to ask about the family business and why they had not prospered but he checked himself. He did not wish to hurt their feelings. Over the next few days, Roshan made visits to his sisters and their families carrying gifts for them. Ram and Mohan accompanied him, thrilled at the chance of taking a jeep ride. There were tearful reunions. The brothers and sisters had always had a special feeling for Roshan, as he was the youngest, and he had never forgotten it. Rukmani, who had treated him like her own child, showed him the nine rakhis she had kept carefully as a symbol of her love—she had observed the festival that is held for brothers every year, hoping to present the sacred strings to him one day. In the short time he was with them, Roshan tried to please his sisters as best he could and gave them all the love he felt. He could not believe he now had nieces and nephews—how lucky he was!

At Madhopur, Roshan made the visits he was dreading—to the homes of Chander and Ramesh. He had told himself he must do it as a mark of respect to his friends. He extended monetary help to both families, saying it was from the sons who would be visiting them soon. He spared them the anguish of knowing the truth. He thought it more prudent to let them lead their lives in hope. But Roshan was amazed that no one in the whole village had any idea of what had happened all those years back in the forest. The incident that had ended his friends' lives and changed his forever had never come to light in spite of the enormity of it! Just as well he thought to let the façade remain and the past be buried.

It was time to return to Shimoga. Roshan had been so involved with his family and friends that the month had flown past quickly. He felt a pang, a sense of regret. He wished he could spend more time at home, but knew he was required to resume his duties and go back to Sethji who would be waiting for him. The circumstances that awaited him at Shimoga, however, were grim. He arrived there to find a sad news. In Roshan's absence Sethji's health had deteriorated and though the doctors had given him their best medical assistance, Sethji passed away before Roshan's return. Furthermore, there was an added turmoil that brewed in the family of the deceased—for in his last will and testament Mallika Arjun had bequeathed his entire empire to Roshan, naming the latter his direct successor. Roshan was shocked. It took him a while to digest the news. The assets in the will meant the ownership of six hundred acres of farmland, a house in Shimoga, two warehouses, one bidi manufacturing factory and three vehicles. Sethji had left him a hefty bank balance as well. Roshan now owned more wealth than he had ever thought possible. Grateful for all that he had been blessed with, Roshan offered obeisance at the same temple where destiny had brought him to Sethji. He prayed for the peaceful passing on of the soul of his mentor.

Mallika Arjun's relatives challenged the will in the district courts and before he could come to terms with the happenings Roshan found himself in the midst of a legal battle. The truth as it stood was that, unknown to Roshan, Sethji had begun to think of him as his own son—he had developed an inexplicable attachment to the young man who had shown the highest regard towards his duties. Making Roshan his designated heir was Sethji's expression of appreciation. There was another thing; Sethji disliked his relatives. He knew they were jealous of his success and were like vultures, waiting with their eyes on his wealth. Roshan was uncomfortable being in the midst of the family battle. He did not consider himself competent enough to fight it. Not knowing what to make of criminal and civil lawyers, he wanted to run home to Madhopur instead. But he resolved to stay. He was a fighter who owed his Sethji this last obligation of carrying out the latter's wishes.

The following months were spent with lawyers and court visits and, eventually, after spending a considerable amount of money and energy, Roshan's efforts paid off. He won the case. Under judicial orders he took complete ownership and charge of Sethji's assets. It was back to business for him. He at once set to work to restore the company's goodwill that had suffered due to the legal imbroglio—the faith of his buyers had to be re-established first, above all else. Thereafter, there was no looking back. Roshan worked harder than ever and created a niche for himself in the markets. With his dedication and effort the tobacco produce increased in profits and his bidi unit grew as well. There was a renewed sense of energy and purpose that drove him to significant breakthroughs. He made new rules and revised the old. He also adopted modern techniques and purchased the latest machinery to back his innovative ideas.

In those years, there was a continuous demand in the developing Indian markets for his areca nut, tobacco and betel leaf, and Roshan capitalized on it by expanding his businesses around these products. The raw materials for his factories of cigarette, bidi and tobacco zarda—a chewing tobacco flavoured with spices—were supplied mostly by his own farms. The bidis of the company were manufactured in the brand name of AP, after Mallika Arjun Pillai, and then Roshan introduced another brand in Sethji's name—Arjun. It was a line of flavoured bidis that became an instant success and created a big demand in the markets of Mysore and the neighbouring states. Roshan's businesses flourished.

By 1960, when he was thirty, Roshan had achieved the kind of wealth and status most people of his age could only dream of. It was time to fulfil a desire he had been harbouring for a very long time—to buy his own family home so he could call his parents and brothers to come and live with him. Roshan bought a large farmhouse, his dream home, and then he wrote a letter addressed to his father and eldest brother, conveying his need for his family and the desire that they live together. Soon after, he brought them to Shimoga. It gave him immense satisfaction to be able to lavish all comforts on them, knowing in his heart how much he had wanted to do this for himself. Now that they were with him, his own life seemed complete in every aspect.

Roshan missed the presence of Seth Mallika Arjun though. He was the person who had made his life. Ever grateful to his benefactor, he had a temple built on his farm and at the entrance to it he had a statue created of Mallika Arjun. Each morning, before the day's work, Roshan would visit this sacred spot to pay his respects.

Roshan also had his employees to thank. They had played a fundamental role in his success and he acknowledged their contribution. He began to share his profits with those who worked for him and gave them bonuses and gifts during festivals. He cared for them, made them happy, and conducted himself as any head of a family would, even though he was much younger than many of his workforce. In the early 1960s, Roshan became the first businessman in Shimoga District to start a welfare scheme for his employees. On a section of his farmland that had grown to almost a thousand acres, he had housing blocks constructed for workers who had no homes. This act of generosity changed the attitude of his people, and they began to view the establishment as their own. There grew a sense of belonging. This resulted in a manifold increase of Roshan's turnover. It reached two crores in 1975.

Roshan had continued to visit the temple that had been his home. He remembered his days of hunger and struggle and the solace he had found within the precincts of the sanctuary. He carried a deep desire to give back in some way and to provide for others who, as he had done, came to the shrine for support. An idea had taken seed in his mind and he decided to bring it to fruition. Taking permission from punditji and the temple trust he began to provide two free meals daily—for up to a thousand poor people—at the park adjacent to the place of worship. Every day crowds thronged there and many came from outside the town. His father questioned the numbers—a thousand people were a lot to take care of. But Roshan, who had never forgotten his struggle, felt it was the least he could do. He told his father that he still remembered the times when the family had gone without eating. Providing food for the hungry was his way of expressing his gratitude for the grace and abundance he had received.

It was in the midst of his business expansions, about a year after his family settled down in Shimoga, that Roshan's parents began to insist that he think of marriage. He had crossed what was considered the conventional age for it, had earned enough to feed generations, and he now needed to seriously think of settling down and having a family of his own. At first Roshan would not hear of it; he did not want to be distracted from his work. But then he remembered Mallika Arjun. He reflected on the life of his benefactor and what the end had been for him. Roshan wondered what he would be earning for if he did not have a family of his own in his later years. The thought changed his mind and he agreed. He was married in Shimoga itself. His bride, Neelima, belonged to the same district.

Roshan was a visionary. In the years that followed he shifted his headquarters to Bombay (now Mumbai), the financial and commercial capital of India, and opened several limited companies. From there he diversified his businesses through various opportunities and also reached, so to speak, the zenith of his commercial triumph. It was the time when the concept of chewing tobacco and paan or betel leaf had begun to change and people had started moving towards paan masala—a blend of nuts, seeds, herbs, spices and flavourings—that was available in small boxes. Roshan diversified and established units for manufacturing his own brand of paan masala. He experimented with various ingredients and after several trials created his own special blend. It was of the finest quality and competitively priced. The product was an instant success. He experimented further and added tobacco to this mixture, and the result was what he called gutka—his unique flagship creation. It took the market by a storm. Roshan now wanted to give his customers a more convenient container in which to carry his products, so he introduced the sachet. It gave people the option of buying paan masala and gutka—in lesser quantities and at a lower price, along with the ease of carrying sachets. He was at his innovative best.

Roshan focused on his leading product. To keep up with market demand, he arranged for a constant supply of bulk raw materials—areca nut, menthol, katha or catechu and lime, in addition to his own production. These were live ingredients. He approached big suppliers in Delhi for these items and managed to have them agree to supply on credit. It was an important achievement for him at this stage. What was more, he also entered into a watertight agreement with his main suppliers—that they would supply to him alone. He wanted monopoly so that he could stay ahead of his competitors.

Roshan opened gutka manufacturing units in many states of India. He made sure that these were located in close proximity to the supply of at least one of the ingredients needed, and he bought two hundred trucks to transport areca nut from his farms to the manufacturing units. Further, he established a pan-India distribution channel. Even though it was a challenge, by this time Roshan had become an influential figure in business circles whose name was a force to reckon with. He had a special network of contacts he could rely on, and taking help now, he set up an intricate supply system. In no time, his products became a household name across the country.

And so it was that Seth Roshan Lal, as he was now known, established his empire of gutka manufacturing. The resultant turnover of his group of companies reached a thousand crores, propelling him into the league of the top ten business houses in India. It was around this time that he was designated Gutka

King. By the time he was seventy, he had further diversified into the businesses of cement, sugar and real estate. He continued to prosper and give several quality products to consumers across India as well as provide employment to thousands of people.

∿

Standing on the riverbank now, lost in his thoughts, Seth Roshan Lal looked at the forest and reminisced. What a long journey it had been—literally from rags to riches! He wondered what his life would have been if he had returned to Madhopur that night from the forest. Fate had willed otherwise. Then he remembered the words of the fakir. Suddenly his thoughts were interrupted by his grandchildren who had come to remind him it was time. The humble king smiled to himself. He gave one last look towards the forest and then he stepped down from the boulder and accompanied his family into the town.

On the grounds outside the town hall a large number of people had gathered and were waiting for their guest of honour, Seth Roshan Lal Maheshwari, to hoist the Indian flag on the Independence Day and later offer sumptuous food to complete the celebrations in the style only the Gutka King could do.

Deceitful Paramour

The taxi halted at the traffic lights. Meena shot a look at the signal, mentally willing it to turn green. She was nervous. She looked at Vikram; he looked back and gave a reassuring nod, all would be well. She smiled back, yes, so long as he was by her side she knew she was safe. The light changed and the driver swerved the vehicle left into the lane leading to the New Delhi railway station. How different she had felt when they had planned this. How romantic it had all seemed. So why this feeling of anxiety now? She tried to compose herself—once they boarded the 4.30 p.m. Rajdhani Express to Mumbai (then Bombay), all would be well.

Meena Seth and Vikram Bakshi had just got married at Laxmi Narayan Temple, popularly known as Birla Mandir, in the area of Connaught Place—the heart of Delhi. The distance to the station was considerably short, but a pulsating urgency loomed over them. Having married secretly, they wanted to get away, to flee the city before their families got wind of the news. And they were running short on time. They had to catch that train!

Mrs Meena Bakshi! The thought sent a warm rush of blood through her being. Meena smiled. Incredible! Her fingers touched her forehead where Vikram had just applied vermillion—the mark of a married Hindu woman. That was all that symbolized the occasion, for the two had deliberately attired themselves casually to avoid drawing attention to themselves. So what! They had a lifetime ahead to create a fantastic wardrobe, thought Meena. She had Vikram and nothing compared with him. She clutched her handbag closer; it held the cash and jewellery she had brought with her to start her new life. What would her mother say when she found the jewellery missing? The thought yanked Meenu back to reality, worrying her once again. What would happen when the two families discovered the extreme step they had taken? How would they react? Meena fought hard to keep those disturbing thoughts away. Besides, why think of the consequences she rationalized with herself—at least for the present she was the happiest person on earth!

The taxi pulled over to the station, minutes before the train was scheduled to depart. Vikram jumped out and Meena followed him. He carried a blue bag in one hand and, taking Meena's hand in the other, he led the way, jostling through the crowd. They ran the distance to platform number two, where their southwest-bound train stood, and dashed into their compartment. They had made it! With a sigh of relief Meena sat back in her seat in the two-tier, air-conditioned coach that Vikram had reserved. He had wanted a coupé in a first class compartment, but none was available. Vikram now looked for the ticket inspector to ask if their reservation could be upgraded to first class. He returned with the information that two stops away, at Ratlam Junction in Madhya Pradesh, a coupe would be available. They could make a shift at that point. The newly married couple settled down by the window of the two lower berths, facing each other. They had combined a small quantity of their belongings—articles they would require on arrival in Mumbai—in Vikram's blue bag. Less luggage meant easier movement. Moreover, considering their escape had been planned in broad daylight, a large suitcase would have been conspicuous. Vikram carefully placed his bag under his seat near the corner, away from sight as it also contained the cash that he had brought along. Meena placed her handbag on the seat beside her. The train began to slowly chug out of the station.

Meena relaxed. She looked at Vikram, and as their eyes met, they smiled, acknowledging the relief they both felt. What a day it had been! But now, for the moment, there was nothing to do but flow with the journey. All thoughts on dealing with life could be dealt with later. They had decided that they would contact their families after settling themselves in the new city. They hoped that by then the parents would have come to terms with the situation and accept them for what could not be reversed.

They shared the compartment with another married couple, a middle-aged man and woman who chattered incessantly. The couple, having settled down on the aisle side of the lower berths, began to engage Meena and Vikram in talk. Vikram did not mind. He answered their questions as it gave him chance to occupy himself in normal conversation. He told them that he and his wife were from Delhi, that he worked in his family business, that they were on their way to Mumbai to meet her parents, and so on. His cordial manner established Meena and him as a regular married couple on a trip. Meena chuckled. No wonder she had fallen for him. He could be very charming when he wanted to.

Evening tea was served and then they had dinner. The passengers began to quieten and settle down for the night. Vikram came and sat by Meena. He held her hand, warm against his. Suddenly the world of the compartment didn't seem to matter. And no one bothered them. He put his arm around her shoulder and, lowering his head, he whispered that their honeymoon had just begun. In response she could only blush. They sat in silence for a while looking out of the window, watching the few scattered lamps of habitation whiz past in the darkness beyond as the train raced on its tracks. Meena felt she couldn't be happier.

Kota Station came and went. The next stop, Ratlam Junction, was still a few hours away; they would arrive there only at midnight. Vikram suggested that they rest till then and he would wake her up at Ratlam so they could move to the first class compartment. Meena tried to convince him to stay where they were, saying that since they were now comfortably settled, there was no need to change coaches. But Vikram insisted. He wanted their privacy as it was their wedding night, he said with a wink. She laughingly agreed. There was no changing Vikram's mind when he was like that. He helped her spread her sheets and lie down before spreading himself out on his berth.

Ratlam Junction came and went. It was a short halt of barely three minutes. No one stirred. When Meena woke up, it was because the train had suddenly jerked. She looked across, Vikram was not on his berth. Maybe he had gone for the switch coaches, she groaned. How she wanted to sleep, to restore the energy she had spent during the day. She lay back waiting, hoping Vikram would change his mind or, better still, the first class coupe would not be available. Minutes ticked by and Vikram was still nowhere in sight. Her watch showed 1.00 a.m. Meena sat up with a start. It was past midnight—where was Ratlam? Was the train running late? She looked at the upper berths; all was quiet as the other passengers slept. Who should she ask? She reached out for the curtains that divided the compartment from the aisle and opened them, but there was no movement on the outside. As she turned back to her berth, she noticed something missing. Her black bag was not there!

She stood rooted. Something was just not right. On immediate impulse she checked for the blue bag. It was there under the berth. But where was Vikram? And where was her bag? Meena started to get worried. With her pulse beginning to pound, she hurried out to the vestibule and woke up the sleeping attendant. Yes, he said, they had crossed Ratlam Junction and no, he had not seen her husband. The ticket collector was at the other end of the train and could only be spoken to at the next station, Vadodara (then Baroda) Junction. They would be there at 3:40 a.m. She wondered why Vikram had not woken her up. Something must have gone wrong, she thought, and felt a dread begin to build inside her. Seeing the look on her face, the attendant agreed to assist. He returned with her to her seat. Maybe the other passengers could help?

The co-passengers of Meena and Vikram were woken up. Had anyone seen Vikram? As the enquiring began, more of those around were woken up. Slowly, a small crowd gathered.

Word began to spread across the compartment and to the neighbouring ones on both sides of the coach. Had anyone seen a tall, fair and handsome young man wearing a blue and white chequered shirt and black trousers? No, no one had.

Suddenly, in the peering crowd, someone looked familiar. Meena looked again and in a flash recognized the face. Spotty! All eyes turned in the direction of her gaze to the dark man in their midst. There was collective mental recoil. He was stout and of medium height, but what caught their attention was his skin condition. It was marked with white patches that were prominent against his natural skin colour. Meena instinctively covered her mouth; she had not meant to shriek that way. Spotty was a lighthearted nickname given to him in college and not meant to offend; but amid the crowd of strangers on the train, it had a different connotation.

Rajesh Kashyap stepped forward and the others immediately made way for him. He was aware of people staring at him but he paid no attention to them. Meena apologized for her reaction; it was just that she had not expected to see him there. She asked where he was headed. He was on a business trip, he told her. He had boarded at Ratlam Junction and was on his way to Mumbai for an important assignment. Vikram Bakshi? Yes, he had seen him on the platform at Ratlam, standing behind a tea stall, watching the train as it left the station. And yes, he carried a black bag. Meena could not believe what she had just heard. Blood rushed to her head and before she could respond, her world collapsed. All turned black as she lost consciousness. For the next few minutes, Meena did not know what happened. She had hit her head against the iron rod holding an upper berth before she fell, and a cut was visible on her forehead from where the blood oozed. There was confusion in the compartment as people buzzed around, not understanding how to take control of the situation. Rajesh stepped in and asserted over the other voices that he knew Meena. They were from the same college. There was no need to worry; he would help her, he declared. He called out if there was a doctor on board. There was. First-aid was given to the bruise on Meena's forehead and she was made to lie on her berth.

When she came to, Meena's head throbbed. Suddenly, she remembered everything and was surprised that she had passed out. Taking the water, she drank slowly, grateful for the liquid that pushed the rising lump back in her throat. Faces stared at her and she wished she could cry. Her mind raced; had Vikram left her? Ditched her? How could he? Questions flooded her mind. What had gone wrong? And why? No! It could not be. It was just not possible. He loved her too much.

She looked at Rajesh. Did he know anything about Vikram? Could he help? Taking the cue, Rajesh sat beside her. His first question was to ask her when the two had got married. He seemed very surprised to know that she and Vikram had come this far. But before she could say anything, he proceeded to tell Meena that it seemed peculiar the way Vikram had stood behind the tea stall, as though he were hiding and waiting for the train to move. And what had caught Rajesh's attention was the look on Vikram's face—there was a smile of triumph. Meena's head swam, she could barely think straight. How could the smart Meena Seth have gone so wrong in her judgement?

The attendant was curious. The others were inquisitive.

Here was a real 70 mm film unfolding before them. They hovered around asking. Why had her husband left her? Did they have a fight? Was there another woman? What would Meena do? They also had many suggestions—she must put in a complaint at the next station, she must call her family, she should not travel alone, and so on. Meena remained shell-shocked. Rajesh politely offered to do what was necessary. He assured Meena of his help and reiterated to those around them that there was no need to feel scared on her account. She was not alone and they, she and he, knew each other. He thanked the passengers for their concern and requested them to return to their berths. Seeing Meena taken care of, there was nothing more for the others to do. Grudgingly, for they would have liked to witness more of the drama, they made their way back to their seats. This was one journey they would be talking about for a long time. Meena was relieved. She could not bear to have prying eyes on her anymore.

Once she was alone with Rajesh, Meena dragged the blue suitcase out from under the berth and opened it. It contained the packet of her belongings that she had handed over to Vikram the day before. There was nothing else. The purport of her situation hit Meena. Yes, Vikram had planned on leaving her! She felt as though she were in quicksand, the ground beneath her giving way with every passing moment. To top it all, she was left with no money to fend for herself. What a predicament! Within hours of her wedding she found herself stranded, abandoned by her husband. She sat still, horrified, totally at a loss at the turn of events. To think that Vikram had left her in that manner and run away with her money and jewellery was absurd. But was this why her brothers Sumit and Vinod had objected to her associating with Vikram? Had they judged him better than she had?

Meena needed time to think about what to do next. One drastic action had backfired and she did not wish to take any other lest she create more problems for herself and her parents. She could not think clearly. Rajesh tried to pacify her. He made Meena comfortable, asked if she needed anything and brought her more water. He was surprised when she told him that Vikram and she had eloped and they had planned to go to Mumbai. As Meena recounted the day's events, the tears she had been controlling began to pour. Trying to collect herself, she told Rajesh she would go to Mumbai by herself. She had a friend who lived there. Maybe she could find some work and begin a new life. Rajesh was quiet. He listened as Meena tried to plan her next steps; then he intervened. He suggested that she get off at Vadodara. It was important, especially now that Vikram had deserted her, that she inform her family and return home. They would be extremely worried. They might even have sent the police in search of her. Meena shuddered. She could not possibly return home. The thought of facing her family filled her with dread. Rajesh offered to help. He requested that she allow him to accompany her. He would escort her to her home in Delhi, and then take a train back to Mumbai.

Meena looked at Rajesh. She was bowled over. How chivalrous of him! Moreover, his suggestion that she return home appealed to logic. That sealed it, and Meena accepted his proposal of escorting her. His compassion gave her the comfort and support she desperately needed. How strange life was! In college she had never paid Rajesh any attention and here he was, literally saving her at her most vulnerable moment. And to think how badly her judgement of Vikram had failed. They alighted at Vadodara Junction and walked to the first class waiting lounge. It was locked. Rajesh had it opened, and leaving Meena there with both the blue bag and the one he carried, he went to enquire about the early morning trains to Delhi.

Left to her thoughts, Meena introspected further. She realized she had committed the biggest blunder of her life by not only running away but also stealing her mother's jewellery and money. By now everyone would have come to know about it. What a letdown for her family in the face of relatives and friends! And what an ungrateful daughter she had proven to be. She would apologize to her parents and brothers a thousand times for putting them through this agony. How could she have mistrusted their judgement, her dear ones who seemed the world to her in this hour of distress. And Rajesh...her saviour... he was God-sent! Rajesh returned holding two small earthen pots of steaming tea. She was grateful. The elixir brought the warmth she so needed. The next train was at 8.45 a.m.—a few hours away, he told her. He had purchased the tickets. He had also booked an urgent trunk call to her home. The overseer of the booth would inform them when the call came through. And when it did come through, it turned out to be a traumatic moment for Meena. If it had not been for Rajesh, her courage would have failed her. He spoke first and introduced himself as a friend who had met her on the train to Mumbai. Mumbai? Meena trembled at the frantic reaction on the other side as the familiar voice of her father carried across. Rajesh managed to convey that she was safe and would be returning home that same evening. He gave the train details and time. Both ends strained to hear, the line being scratchy. Her brother came on next and asked to speak to her. Meena answered, half crying and apologetic. She had a lot to tell but could not do so on call. She would explain everything when she was back home. Yes, she was fine, and there was nothing to worry about...and then the line disconnected.

Meena and Rajesh returned to the waiting room. Meena was exhausted, but she couldn't sleep. She sat staring blankly into space. Rajesh stretched himself out as best as he could, looked at her and asked her a question. When did Meena and Vikram meet? She stared at him as though woken up from a stupor. It took her a few minutes, and then her mind jolted back to the time she had come to Delhi from Allahabad. It all seemed such a long time ago. She braced herself and began her story...

Meena lived in Allahabad during her school days. Her father had wanted her to go to Delhi University for her higher education, so she had joined college there. Meena remembered how excited she had been about studying in the capital. In Delhi she stayed with her uncle—an IRS officer and a senior bureaucrat—at his house in Shah Jahan Road.

Meena was a confident girl. Attractive, charming, vivacious and carefree, she was liked by everyone. Her father was a rich businessman. He had a flourishing apparel business in Allahabad and Lucknow while her uncle in Delhi, an income tax commissioner, was no less. He was wealthy, influential and was known to be quite shrewd. He owned properties near Kanpur and Agra, and these yielded a high rental income.

In the monsoon of 1975, when Delhi University commenced its new session after the summer vacations, Meena began her first year course in English Literature at Miranda House. It was the start of a new life in the city. Meena led an enviable lifestyle. Her uncle indulged her to make up for having no daughter of his own. She wore the latest in fashion trends and carried herself well. A chauffeur-driven car remained at her disposal at all times. She also had an unending reservoir of pocket money—deep enough to afford treats for her friends and batch mates every other day. Together they watched the latest movies or dined out, and Meena loved to oblige because she basked in the attention she got. In no time she became a popular figure in college. She played basketball and was inducted into the college team in her first year itself. Soon the entire college knew Meena and that she belonged to an influential family with significant connections. She was a favourite of the staff as well and of a particular liking to her games instructor.

When she was in her third year of college, Meena's games instructor organized a practice match for her team with the boys of a neighbouring college. Meena was to lead her team as the captain. She was apprehensive about playing with boys; her team would be thrashed to pulp, she thought. They had heard about the players of the opposing side who were one of the best in the state. And one of those players was Vikram Bakshi, the captain of the boys' team. Vikram Bakshi was famous in the university and one of the best looking in the campus. To the smitten girls he was a Greek god—tall, chiselled features, well-built, athletic. But Meena eyed him as a 'challenge'. Famous as a stunner herself, with her fair share of besotted boys clamouring for her attention, she wondered with a laugh how long it would be before Vikram bowed to her charm. So what if her team lost, she thought, at least there would be another name added to her list of admirers. She shared her thoughts with her friend Kavita and they looked forward to the match for more reasons than just winning it.

Vikram Bakshi loved his game, and as the match progressed he put his best into it. He seemed to barely notice her, except for the formality of acknowledging his counterpart. It was a great match, drawing a massive crowd as all matches between the opposite sexes in college are known to do. The girls, predictably lost, but the crowd whistled and applauded; but for which side, no one knew. At the end of it, Meena faced the greatest shock of her life—it was she who had fallen madly for Vikram. In the coming days Meena came to her wits' end. Vikram's behaviour puzzled her. Spoilt with the attention she normally attracted, she refused to believe that he had not noticed her. Kavita advised her to remain calm, for Vikram would surely contact her. Boys were strange and sometimes they took their time in expressing their feelings. But Meena was not used to waiting. She began visiting his college and once sent a note proposing another match, but there was no response. Eventually, losing patience, Meena took the plunge and dialled his hostel number from a public telephone booth. Vikram was summoned by his hostel attendant and after a long wait he received Meena's call. She invited him to meet her at the coffee house of Law Faculty. He accepted her invitation.

She sat in the coffee house waiting for over two hours but Vikram did not show up. Thankfully, Meena had kept her plan of meeting Vikram a secret; she had not confided even to Kavita. She was now glad she would be saved the embarrassment of explaining that Vikram had stood her up. Badly let down, she was more determined than ever to meet him. It was not easy. Communication was difficult as the attendants at the boys' hostel were not always willing to look for students to receive calls. Also, barring calls from their homes, the boys were strictly discouraged to receive telephonic calls from any other source. Days passed. Meena was desperate, but more than that she was intrigued. She could not fathom Vikram's behaviour. He had clearly accepted her offer, and then to not show up...what could it mean? Was he being arrogant? Playing hard-to-get? And he had not so much as called or sent a message to apologize for his absence. Kavita suggested she forget the whole matter. What? Meena forget a boy for shunning her? Unthinkable!

And then one day she had a chance encounter with Vikram at a well-known restaurant. He was hosting a lavish party for his friends. He invited her to join his group along with her friends. Seeing the look of bewilderment on her face, he apologized profusely. It was a long story he said. He would explain some other time why he had not contacted her, but he requested her to please believe his best intentions. Could she join in and help him make up for annoying her? It was enough to melt Meena's heart—pining as she was for him. Besides, she wondered what her batch mates accompanying her would think. Would they not be impressed—for Meena was being invited by *the* Vikram? She considered herself very lucky, for Vikram seemed to be a rich boy. Afterwards, he offered to drop her off at her uncle's house. Meena's heart did a double-take. Here he was ignoring her on one hand while on the other he knew where she lived. She excused herself from her friends saying she needed to discuss the next match urgently with Vikram. Giving instructions to her driver to drop the girls off, she herself accepted Vikram's offer. What a treat it was she thought! What more could a girl ask for?

In the waiting room, Meena had a faraway look in her eyes as, for a moment, she relived the experience of her first drive with Vikram in his car—a sleek black Fiat in the latest model that outshone her uncle's old Ambassador. Sitting beside the most sought-after hunk in the university, only because he had asked her, was for Meena the ultimate! During the drive, Vikram told her about his family.

Here Meena stopped. She had caught a puzzled look on Rajesh's face. All along her reverie he had been quiet…did she lose him somewhere? Rajesh asked her to repeat what Vikram had said about his family. She did. Vikram had told her of his father's businesses in Chandigarh, their sprawling bungalow in one of the aristocratic sectors of the city, their exclusive lifestyle and their frequent travels abroad. Rajesh refuted it all. Those were all lies! Meena felt a chill run through her spine as she heard the truth that Vikram belonged to a very ordinary family. His father worked as an accountant for a well-known business tycoon in Chandigarh who owned showrooms and a chain of hotels in that part of the country. The lifestyle he spoke of belonged to the tycoon, not his father!

Poor Meena gulped. This was getting too much for even her strong disposition to take. She did not know how to go on. When the foundation itself was rendered false, how could the rest of what she had to say stand? However, Rajesh goaded her to do so. She did, but now her tone had changed.

It was their second outing—her first proper date with Vikram. How foolishly impressed she had been when he nonchalantly tossed the car keys at the valet and escorted her to the most expensive five-star hotel—nothing less would do for her, he had said. She had brought up the topic of his ignoring her earlier, as they sat down at their table at the Chinese restaurant, but Vikram had brushed it off with a light apology, making nothing of it. He had then presented her with a chic Omega watch to mark the occasion. She had tried to resist but he would not hear of it. His style and his bearing were overwhelming; she could just not refuse. The story was forgotten. By the end of that meal, Meena was sold. She was impressed by his chivalry, the way he articulated himself and his level of confidence. Vikram literally swept her off her feet. He was perfect. And she, hopelessly in love!

It was only now that she wondered how he could have bought the Omega. It was a very expensive piece; no one in her college wore one. How proud she had felt...and how vain! How could an accountant's son have afforded it? She wished she had asked him then.

At that time she could not have suspected anything untoward. He had seemed the most thoughtful person, taking care of her every need and respecting her space. She had curfew timings to adhere to and Vikram proved a responsible person— always dropping her home by 8.00 p.m. and avoiding late-night movies because her uncle would not approve of it. He was careful never to put Meena in any kind of trouble. What was more, only their closest friends knew about their frequent dates.

They were careful, as even a small rumour spread like wildfire across the campus. Vikram did not want her to have to face that.

Meena now bitterly remembered the times they had spent together and the exotic places he had taken her to—the movies, the dining out, the discotheques in the afternoons, and even shopping—he had given her some very expensive gifts. She wished she had asked him 'how'? But how could she have when she had lost her senses, having been completely swept away by his panache, not to mention the fragrance of his aftershave. Rajesh quietly broke into her thoughts. The car Vikram took her around in was his, he said. Meena stared at him in disbelief. Her thoughts went back to the time she had seen Rajesh for the first time. It had surprised her. The white patches, his less-than-average looks, his ordinary persona...how could Vikram have a friend like him? But Vikram had called Rajesh a nice person and that had impressed Meena about Vikram. It fit the picture. Vikram hung around with him because Rajesh was known to be rich. She knew it because he had once come with his father to meet her uncle for a tax matter. She had disliked the way he had looked at her then, more so because of his own looks. But being used to boys staring at her, she had not given it another thought.

Rajesh wondered when it was that she and Vikram had decided to elope. What was the need to do so? Could they not have talked to their parents and told them about their feelings for each other? Meena hesitated. Her thoughts went to that special evening when she and Vikram were watching a movie. How could she tell Rajesh? They had held hands before, but this time they were very close. They were on the last row of seats

and Vikram had leaned forward and kissed her. And after the
movie when they were walking to the car parking, it had begun
to drizzle. They ran to avoid getting wet and dived into the car
laughing. She suddenly found Vikram watching her quietly as
she brushed the droplets of water from her hair; then he shifted
closer and tried to kiss her again. Meena had moved back, a
little flustered. Was she ready for this? Sensing her hesitation,
Vikram had withdrawn himself. Then he had started the engine
and driven the car towards Shah Jahan Road in silence.

Meena could not sleep that night. Her thoughts kept going
back to Vikram's kiss. How she wanted to be with him. They
made the best couple, she thought, and he too was from a
rich family like hers. But they were only in the third year of
college. Maybe they could get engaged, complete their studies
and then get married. Perhaps Vikram had been in a similar
state of mind, for in their next meeting, he proposed to her.
No, she could not possibly tell Rajesh how close she had been
with Vikram and how the two of them had badly wanted to
get married and be with each other. What would Rajesh think?
She barely knew him if not for the train journey.

Now, looking at Rajesh, she told him how Vikram's and
her life changed when Vinod saw them with each other. Events
unfolded so dramatically that they had no alternative but to run
away. It was one evening when Vikram was dropping her off
at the gate that her cousin happened to see them. On hearing
of it her uncle had been alarmed. He had immediately made a
call to Allahabad and her parents had rushed to Delhi. Meena's
parents had refused to listen to her. They forbade her from
meeting Vikram. They did not want her meeting boys they did

not know about. She had put up some resistance, and seeing this behaviour they forbade her from going out altogether—not even with her girlfriends. Except for her going to college, she was mostly confined to the walls of the house. She hated her cousin and vowed never to help him again when he wanted to go out with girls.

After a week, Meena's father had returned to Allahabad but her mother stayed on. It was January, 1978. Meena's final examination in April was only a few months away, so it was decided that once Meena was done with her papers, she and her mother would return to Allahabad together. In addition, there was to be a family wedding in Delhi in February and her mother was delighted that she could now easily attend the functions.

For Meena, as though Vinod was not enough to keep vigilance over her, her brother Sumit in Allahabad was given instructions to visit Delhi every fortnight in case his mother required any help. Now both Vinod and Sumit, when in town, kept a vigil on Meena, and she hated it. But Meena was not one to be restrained, especially without reason, as she believed. She began to hatch her own plot. Taking her closest friend Kavita's help, she met Vikram after college and confronted him. Was he serious about her? Would he marry her immediately? Vikram tried to pacify her. Yes, he was serious, but he did not wish to act hastily. He suggested she remain quiet for the moment. His parents were to visit him next month and he would ask them to speak with her parents. They would surely get the approval of the elders. And once they had completed their college education and he had established himself in his father's business, they would get married. But he insisted that she must keep patience or everything would be lost.

Rajesh interrupted Meena. Those were excuses, he said. Maybe Vikram did not want marriage. But, argued Meena, he had seemed most serious. Rajesh did not think so—Vikram could not possibly have been serious about Meena, for he was seeing other girls as well. Meena thought she would collapse. She must get some fresh air She stood up and walked slowly out onto the platform. The time of dawn was quiet and peaceful and it soothed Meena's nerves. After a few minutes, Rajesh followed her. Meena turned to him and enquired about the 'other girls'—who were they? Rajesh asked her to complete her story first.

Meena continued recalling with a sense of disgust how, after a few days, Vikram had sent her a message to meet him after college. He told her that he had had a word with his parents and they were not keen on the alliance. They wanted him to settle into the family business first. They also had another girl in mind for him. Vikram had said that there was no other way out but to get married secretly on the day of their last examination. Meena was to leave for Allahabad the day after. Strangely, he mentioned not telling even their closest friends. He wanted to play it very safe—in case word leaked out. The reason was all too clear now, thought Meena. His intentions were never honourable. What was more, he had said they must carry whatever money or jewellery they could as they were not going to get any assistance from their parents. Vikram had then made the train reservations.

On the day of her penultimate examination, Meena had handed over her packet of clothes to Vikram to be carried in his bag. And then on that fateful day of the last examination, in the morning itself, she had taken out the cash from her mother's cupboard as well as the jewellery her mother had worn at her wedding. She would not notice till the next day when they were to leave Delhi, Meena thought. In the afternoon, after her paper, she had met Vikram at Laxmi Narayan Temple. She had carried her treasure in her black bag while he had supposedly brought whatever money he could in his blue bag along with her packet. After getting married they had rushed to the railway station to catch the train to Mumbai.

Meena returned to the waiting room and sat down. She felt ill. Rajesh brought more tea and sandwiches and sat down beside her. Meena wondered where Vikram could have gone. Her family, especially Sumit and Vinod, would not spare him, she said. They were influential people and it would not take them long to trace him. But the most important thing she felt was to know the reason behind such behaviour. Maybe he would apologize and all would be well. Rajesh was alarmed—how could she think so even after how Vikram had treated her? Vikram's character was now exposed, he said, so Meena must not think of going back to him. Rajesh said he could never imagine that she and Vikram had wanted to get married. In fact, he could never believe that Vikram could be serious about any girl because he changed relationships ever so often. Rajesh further added that Vikram was also in the habit of borrowing money. He would take money from people and not return it. Probably that was how he had afforded the gifts and outings with Meena. He was a true con man—one who lived a life of lies and deceit. Rajesh was sure Vikram had led other girls astray too and duped them of their money and jewellery. Very few people knew the real Vikram, Rajesh said. He himself had stopped associating with him once he understood Vikram's real character.

Meena was in tears. She wept uncontrollably. Rajesh left her alone for a while and went to enquire if their train was running on schedule. At 8.45 a.m. they boarded the train to Delhi. Broken, bewildered and not in the right state of mind, Meena was only too relieved to have Rajesh take control of the situation.

∾

Meena Kashyap stood at the window of her sixth floor office in Mayur Bhawan in Connaught Place, looking out at the horizon and the street below. Everything had changed in the last so many years. And to think it had all begun not very far from where she stood in her office building—at Laxmi Narayan Temple! Could she ever forget that train ride, and how midway, her destination, in fact her destiny, had changed! Vadodara. The waiting room. The return...

In June 1978, two months after that eventful journey, Meena married Rajesh Kashyap in a simple ceremony. She wanted the affair to be a small and private one, and Rajesh had understood her feelings. However, a get-together was held the same evening to announce the wedding to their families and business associates. Meena's father and uncle had a large circle of contacts whom they wished to extend their courtesies to. She remembered people observing, puzzled and curious, at the strange couple the two made. She, the ravishing young bride, and he, the gawky and unpleasant groom. No one knew the real story. No one was to be told.

On their return that evening from Vadodara, much had transpired in the residence at Shah Jahan Road. Rajesh had warned her on the journey back—she must not say much. She had erred badly in her judgement. It may not have been entirely her fault, for Vikram was a charmer, yet there was no reason for her to worry her family anymore. She had let them down already. He had also suggested that the family should not be given complete information of her affair with Vikram or his real character be divulged. The lesser told, the lesser the questions. Meena had agreed. The details were to remain between her and Rajesh.

Meena had hung her head in humiliation and apologized profusely to her elders. But it was hard for them to accept what had happened. They were distraught. Had they not given her everything she needed? How could she have done this to them?

In hindsight, Meena gave most of the credit for controlling the situation to Rajesh. He had handled it deftly, explaining how he knew Vikram and what the latter was capable of, that anyone in Meena's shoes would have fared worse, that Meena meant well for her family, and so on. Fortunately, as it happens in close families, the parents came around. Once the initial reactions had cooled off and tempers had settled, they heaved a sigh of relief—their daughter was back, safe! Then the matters of concern that loomed over them were addressed. The first was what the extended families and others should be told if they asked, but that was an easy one to handle. It was the second and graver concern that troubled them. Their daughter was now married, how were they to undo that? Should they report the matter to the police? Where could they find Vikram? Should they forget about everything and carry on with life? What if Meena were to marry someone in the future and Vikram returned? Then what? There were no answers.

They continued to talk till late, Rajesh having joined them for dinner. His conduct had a positive influence on them. He was well-mannered and well-spoken, and they took an immediate liking to him. They could not stop thanking him for bringing Meena home. If it had not been for him, they said, anything could have happened to her. He left after dinner. As for Meena, no one had asked how she felt. For the next few days, the one question that haunted the family was what to do about Vikram. They did not wish to report him as that would bring tremendous shame on the family. They had a reputation to protect. Rajesh visited them every day. In the current matter that troubled them, Rajesh assumed the status of family. He was consulted for every idea or thought.

In those days, Meena came to depend upon Rajesh. She shared her feelings and confided in him. They were united in a secret that no one else knew of. Slowly, she began to feel closer to him, looking forward to the times he would visit so they could talk. It lightened her heart. Vinod, her cousin, was the first to notice this. He saw the increasing reliance his sister had begun to have on Rajesh and the growing bond between the two. One day, as the family sat together, he suggested that they get Meena married to Rajesh. Everyone looked at each other. Yes, it seemed like the most sensible thing to do. Rajesh knew all about Vikram. Even if Vikram were to return, Meena would be safe. And then Rajesh seemed to think well of Meena. But would he agree? That evening, Rajesh was asked for his consent to marry Meena. He was willing. He expressed that he could never have dreamt of marrying someone like her and that it would be an honour for him to do so; but only if she agreed too. Did she have a choice? Meena was too numb to think. But she consoled herself; Rajesh had proved to be true. And by agreeing to marry her, he had demonstrated once more that he could be depended upon. She did like him. To marry him seemed the best, if not the only way out of the current circumstances.

Post their wedding, Rajesh had taken Meena to Switzerland. And so she had begun a life she had always dreamt of with Vikram. Rajesh proved to be a loving husband and he took care of Meena as best as he could. As the years passed by, she had two lovely children, a loving home, and a husband who still doted on her. Meena had no cause for complaint.

Time progressed and she did too. In the dawn of the new millennium, Meena Kashyap was promoted to the rank of Director of Income Tax (Investigation). Her honesty and straightforward dealings became well known in the departments. She was a figure to be reckoned with. No one messed with her work, nor dared to influence her decisions in any way. Her reputation of working in the interest of the government was well established.

Involved as she was with clearing out the black market, with her new position she wielded greater power to press on. She was an example of the adage: 'With seniority comes responsibility resulting in further devotion towards one's work.' She was determined to expose hoarders of black money and promised herself not to rest until she had cleaned the system out. No unfair dealing escaped her experienced eye, and she became famous for her intelligent handling of search and seizure matters.

As fate would have it, that same year an honest Indian banker was posted at Zurich Bank in Switzerland. He noticed that a large number of Indians had undisclosed accounts in Swiss banks. Out of a total of 3500 account holders, one-third were Indians. He prepared a list of the Indian names, and at an opportune time, sent this list to the chairman of Central Board of Direct Taxes (CBDT) in New Delhi. The chairman called a high-powered meeting and asked his team, which included Meena, to conduct an enquiry into the accounts. Meena took the list and went over it. The name at serial number 736 caught her attention—Vikram Bakshi of Gandhi Nagar in Surat, Gujarat. She stopped. Could he be the same Vikram, she wondered? She decided that she would investigate.

Standing tall as Meena Kashyap now did at the window of her office, that was the name that had triggered in her mind memories of the days after that train journey. Vikram Bakshi— she had not forgotten him even after twenty-two years. How could she?

Meena now read the initial report tabled by her assistants. It stated that the person named Vikram Bakshi had opened a diamond manufacturing unit in Surat in 1981 and the current turnover was eighty-five crore rupees. The figure was way too impressive for a son of an accountant to have achieved, thought Meena. It needed more evidence. She instructed her assistants to give it a thorough search. If her colleagues and subordinates wondered why Meena had her focus on that particular serial number when there were bigger fishes with deposits of several thousand crores, they did not show it. She must have her reasons, they thought. But even Meena was in for a surprise. Further investigations revealed that in around 1981, Vikram had been provided with a loan of rupees twenty-five lakh by the Bank of Saurashtra in Gujarat. He had gone on to establish a business in diamond manufacturing by the name of RECO Diamonds Industries Ltd in the industrial area of Surat. In ten years' time, he had managed a turnover that touched six crores and this had risen manifold to the figure in the current financial year. On the surface of the report that was the main information given, there was not much otherwise. It seemed another success story of a poor but hard-working person having made it big by the sheer dint of his toil. But it was the distressing details that rendered Meena off-balance. She gasped! The person who acted as guarantor when Vikram Bakshi got the initial loan from Bank of Saurashtra was Rajesh Kashyap.

Her husband!

That was in 1981. And although the overdraft limit and term loans had grown to bigger sums, the guarantor remained the same till the current year. Meena baulked. Her husband? The guarantor for the most hated man in her life? What was this? She read and re-read the report several times. It also stated that Rajesh Kashyap was the guarantor of Vikram Bakshi in the sales tax department. She could not digest it. There was more. The report also mentioned that Vikram and Rajesh had met at Luxembourg and Zurich a month back. Meena was aware of Rajesh's frequent trips to Switzerland but she had no inkling that he had met Vikram there. What was Rajesh hiding from her? She was now desperate to know.

Meena closed the file. She tried to recall from over the years...had she missed something she ought to have seen? She had never interfered with her husband's extremely successful automobile business or his other ventures. He had never given her any cause for complaint either. A loving husband and father, Rajesh had been by her side all along. To think that he had helped Vikram get such a large contract and then to have kept the information from her was impossible to comprehend. She was determined—she must get to the bottom of it. Meena made a telephone call to her counterpart at the FEMA office at Akbar Road in New Delhi and roped him in to investigate the foreign accounts angle of the two men in her life. Her colleagues, this time, expressed their concern. Why would she want to investigate her husband and his business establishments when he had no direct link with Vikram whose records were under scrutiny anyway? Meena mustered all her courage to answer. She reasoned with her co-workers. They held office of a sensitive nature, she explained. If at any point an investigation led to a spouse or a relative, would they close the case or would they continue to try and reach a logical end? The answer was evident.

Was it a personal fight? Or was she being impartial by not turning a blind eye? Meena did not know. All she knew was that she had gone too far into the matter to let go of it now. And confronting Rajesh Kashyap would achieve little. She decided to leave him to the course of the law. But he was her husband! A decision in that regard would have to be taken and, painful as it was going to be, she would have to face it. Meena braced herself for the days to come. Additional investigations led to more disturbing revelations. A report by the Intelligence Bureau exposed fresh meetings and business talks between Rajesh and Vikram. A diary of Rajesh that was seized contained the details of his Swiss bank account number as well as the details of his transfer of funds through money laundering to an account maintained by Vikram in St Kitts.

No wonder then, thought Meena, the reason for Rajesh's encouragement of her to pursue a career in the Indian Revenue Service. She had always been fascinated by the subject, having watched her uncle perform his duties, and how Rajesh had insisted that she take it up. Did he think it would be a cover-up for all his deeds? Bit by bit, the puzzle began to fall into place for Meena. The black Fiat that Rajesh had given Vikram had been only the beginning. Vikram's gifts to her and his lavish spending had been part of the deal that Rajesh had had with him. Vikram had only been playing the role of the pawn all along. He, who had needed money badly, must have been paid handsomely by Rajesh for his service to him. Now that she was piecing it together, it all made sense...

Rajesh's timely appearance on the train—his description of Vikram on the platform at Vadodara...how meticulously the plan had rolled! They had made sure of leading Meena into a miserable corner from where she had had no escape but to take help and Rajesh had assumed the role of a saviour. Her mind, now matured to think through layers, asked how Rajesh could have bought tickets for their return journey in the middle of the night...it was impossible. It must all have been pre-planned. Further, the smooth talker had won the hearts of her family.

Rajesh's objective from the very beginning had been Meena Seth, and how to make her his own. He would have gauged her interest in Vikram and moved in to take Vikram's place, knowing he himself could never have her, not even in his wildest dreams. It had never been Vikram. It had been Rajesh plotting and planning his deceit all along!

A month later, the Income Tax Department (Investigation), with more than two hundred officials and policemen, landed at Rajesh Kashyap's auto parts factory in Mumbai and offices in Delhi. There were instructions by the top brass in the CBDT to show no leniency towards him, to unearth all the black money and book the culprit under the various provisions of the enactments. In the 963-page appraisal report prepared by the investigation wing of the Income Tax Department in New Delhi along with the investigation wing in Ahmedabad, it was revealed that Vikram, still unmarried, had been sending gifts to a woman at Naya Nagar in Surat. This address was covered as a consequential raid and a sum of fifteen crores was unearthed from the boot of a car parked in the garage. The car was a gift too from Vikram to her.

Rajesh and Vikram were arrested for money laundering under the Foreign Exchange Management Act (FEMA) of 2000. They also faced prosecution for violation of the law and owning bank accounts in St Kitts and Zurich without informing the Reserve Bank of India and the concerned government authorities. They were sentenced to rigorous imprisonment for seven years.

The evening before the arrest, Meena left Delhi for some urgent work in Mumbai.

On the morning of the arrest, Rajesh dialled his wife's mobile number. It was impossible! It was *his* game, he thought, so how could Meena give him a checkmate? She could not have exposed him. But there was no answer.

That same morning in Mumbai, Meena stood on the sands of Juhu Beach, looking at the vast stretch of the sea. The irony of it all, she thought. Just when she had caught up with the men in her life, she had lost them. Surprisingly, she felt no pain. As she watched the frolic around her, a thought brought a fleeting smile to her face. She looked at her watch. It was almost time. Her children were arriving by the morning flight from Delhi to join their mother. Spurred on by the fresh sea breeze, she turned, and holding her head high she walked towards the city to begin her life once again.

Train to Wagah

It was the first monsoon of the new millennium. The twentieth century had passed on the baton to the twenty first. The flight from Mumbai to Srinagar took two and half hours. Hazy yet scenic landscapes and myriad smudged colours of the flora met our eyes through the wet panes of the craft before we touched down. The temperature was 14 °C in Srinagar, and compared to the summer heat and humidity of Mumbai, the weather was excellent. It was hard to believe that barely two hours away from my home, I was in the midst of Kashmir Valley with snow-peaked mountains of the Himalayan ranges encircling the beautiful vista. Set like a bejewelled crown on the map of India, Kashmir is a multifaceted diamond, changing its colours with every season.

Srinagar, the enchanting capital of Jammu and Kashmir, is a slice of Paradise on Earth—the befitting name the Mughals gave Kashmir. A beauty unparalleled, the city is a delight to behold. Picturesque rippling lakes and rolling gardens against the Pir Panjal Range leave one spellbound even as honey-dew fruit orchards and Chinar trees, an integral part of the place, beckon every soul to witness the charms of this valley.

From the airport, Suhail, my business associate, and I engaged a taxi to take us to our destination. It was a slow drive due to the rain. The clouds were dark, and it seemed the incessant downpour was hell-bent on further raising the Jhelum River that was already flowing at the danger level.

We had made arrangements to spend two weeks at Suhail Malik's luxurious bungalow—Rawalpura House at Sanat Nagar in Srinagar. Well-furnished, well-equipped and with a beautiful, sprawling garden filled with the blossoms of the season, the house was built in the 1970s by Suhail's grandfather. The latter had been posted at the Northern Command in Kashmir and, after having fallen in love with the pure beauty and mesmerizing charm of this stunning place, he had decided to stay on in the valley. We, sadly, were not to have much time to enjoy the comforts of the home as we were in Srinagar on business. Both our families had their origins in Pakistan. Suhail's family belonged to Peshawar and I was born in Lahore in February 1947, just before the partition. Presently, being in the carpet business, we had come to Kasimir to explore the possibilities of finding new vendors and manufacturers. 'Progressive businessmen' is what we called ourselves. For many years now, my father had been purchasing carpets from Kashmir, and our brand name—Gulmarg Carpets—enjoyed tremendous goodwill in Mumbai where we had our large showrooms at Crawford market and Linking Road.

But even as we settled down, I began to experience that same strange feeling I always did when I visited Kashmir. I had always been enchanted by the valley, but whether it was the beauty of the place or a certain strange and very strong feeling that had a grip on me, I could not tell.

The next day we drove to the Kashmir Handloom Emporium at Lal Chowk. It was a balmy and cheerful morning—an ideal condition for a long drive in the valley. The clouds had parted, allowing sunshine to cast its glitter on Srinagar's beautiful iconic setting—the sparkling Dal Lake with its colourful boats called shikaras and the houseboats parked along its periphery. We lowered the windows to let the gentle breeze brush our faces, enjoying every bit of the visual treats gliding past us.

At the emporium, the manager introduced us to a tall and smart-looking manufacturer and supplier of carpets, Usman Ali. He was courteous and on the recommendation of the manager, he took us along with him to see his business unit situated on the outskirts of Srinagar on the road leading to Gulmarg. Along the way, he briefed us on the carpet business and current manufacturing trends in the region. Usman Ali showed his impressive factory and, thereafter, invited us to join him for lunch there itself. In the midst of enjoying my favourite Gustaba, a famous traditional Kashmiri delicacy, we conversed about the political situation in Kashmir. I mentioned that my forefathers originally belonged to Pakistan and that I was from Lahore. Usman Ali, in turn, spoke about how a lady called Ayesha Begum had lived with his family for a long time as a chaperone to his kid sisters. She was from Lahore too. I was curious. I asked our host if he had any further information about her; where in Lahore she had lived and the family she belonged to. Usman Ali mumbled something about a Raja Ram Street near Anarkali Bazaar and I dropped the piece of food I was holding in my fingers! I was not being clumsy but the mention of the street took its toll. What a coincidence! My family had lived in house number five on the same street I blurted out within an amazed expression.

I did not remember my mother who we believed had died during the partition mayhem, but I had always prayed that someday I would hear of more details and come to know exactly what had happened to her. Due to this unfulfilled desire any mention of Lahore always caught my attention. In the days after partition, my father had searched the refugee camps at Punjab and Delhi. He had not only given advertisements in newspapers but had also made several trips to Amritsar and Ludhiana in search of my mother. One time, he was even sent on a wild goose chase by a swami, a self-professed godman, who claimed to be able to reunite families separated during the partition. During the early sixties, after relocating to Mumbai from Delhi, my father had made one last desperate attempt to look for my mother across the border. He had visited Lahore and he met some of his old acquaintances to make enquiries. But he could not obtain any worthwhile information. Millions were done to death and probably she was one of them. I remember sitting on my balcony at Juhu in Bombay, watching the sun set and hoping that when my father returned she would be with him...but that was not to be. In my early years, I missed the pampering and affection typically showered by mothers and was jealous of my friends who had that love. I prayed that I too be given, if only for one day, the love of my mother.

My thoughts were interrupted by our host who brought me back to the present. I apologized profusely. But it was too close even for a coincidence. My host was stating that his father, Mir Qasim Ali, had been kind and had sympathized with Ayesha Begum. He and his wife Salma had needed somebody to take care of their three children and hence had requested her to work as a chaperone to them. She had stayed with Salma as her best friend and a guardian to her children. Usman Ali remembered her living with them till the time he was sent to London to study business management at Oxford University. I asked if it was possible to meet Ayesha Begum. He advised me to finish my lunch and then he would make enquiries about her. After the meal, Usman Ali suggested we return to the city to his residence. He hoped his wife would be able to help us in the matter or, maybe, the other servants in his house would have some information about Ayesha Begum's whereabouts.

The door of Usman Ali's bungalow was opened by their trusted old servant. He seated Suhail and me in the living room before heading to the upper floor to notify the landlady of the house. Usman Ali's wife was suave and sophisticated. After making us comfortable, she told us that her husband had acquainted her with the purpose of our visit and had asked her to make enquiries about the chaperone. She further told me that Ayesha Begum's residence had been in the outhouse and that she had left after Usman Ali's mother had passed away. She herself had come to the house much later and had never known the chaperone personally. It was found from the other helpers in the house that Ayesha Begum had started living at a religious place—a temple situated at a short distance from Srinagar—known as the 'Kheer Bhawani Temple'. I thanked the lady sincerely and immediately set off for the place without wasting any more time. I had a strong hunch that I was on the right trail this time and would soon be meeting someone who could finally throw some light on my mother's disappearance on the fateful night of 11 August 1947.

Mir Qasim Ali and Salma had passed away many years ago and Usman Ali had never been given the details of the woman who had lived with them for almost forty years. He had been away from Kashmir for a long time and had returned after the passing away of his father. By then, Ayesha Begum had left their home and had settled down somewhere on the outskirts of Srinagar. I remembered a very old photograph. It was torn at the corners but kept carefully intact by my father. It showed my mother standing with him in the verandah of our house in Lahore. Father held me in his arms. The expression of happiness and pride on the faces of both my parents was apparent. The photograph was taken in June 1947 when I was four months old. I was wrapped in linen clothing and could barely be seen, but my mother's face with her large and beautiful eyes, her prominent cheek bones and a long sharp nose was clearly visible. She wore traditional attire—a salwar kameez with an embroidered green zari dupatta. My father and I would look at that lone picture we had—he remembering her affectionately, and I, trying to imagine the person she would have been. I revered her in that photograph. It was the only link we had with her and was our prized possession.

My father had told me several times that I had been very lucky to have miraculously escaped the pre-partition riots. The uprising had reached a frightening peak by July and August in 1947 when thousands of men, women and children had been massacred. Many from my closest families became victims of the partition. At that time I, Rahul, was the only child of a young Sham Sunder Seth of twenty-one years and his wife Roshini Seth who was only nineteen years old. On 11 August 1947, a group of fanatics entered my grandfather Rai Bahadur Sant Lal Seth's shop at Anarkali Bazaar and set it ablaze. The old servant Lal Singh, unable to save himself from the assault of the armed mob, perished in the fire. The crowd later gathered outside the haveli-style home of Rai Bahadur. He had lost his wife to illness only a few months ago and, at that time, he and his four daughters were present at home. The mob shouted slogans as they surrounded the haveli and hurled stones and blazing torches over the outer stone wall into the courtyard of the house. Rai Bahadur and his daughters tried to fortify themselves as best as they could. They locked the doors of the main building of the three-storied house and sealed the windows. Crouching against an opening on an upper floor, they watched as the mob set fire to the high wooden gates at the outer wall. They knew that once the outer barricade was down, it was only minutes before the frenzied crowd would cross the front courtyard and attack the door of the main building. Rai Bahadur realized the danger and feared his daughters were no longer safe. In that instant, he chose the extreme action.

The well from where they drew water for drinking and washing purposes lay at the back of the house. Rai Bahadur now faced his daughters—there was no escape, he entreated; the only way to save themselves from the fanatics outside was to take their own lives. As the house was set on fire and flames began to spread, the girls knew their fate. They embraced each other for the last time and jumped into the well to meet their tragic end. The youngest was only fourteen then. Rai Bahadur Sant Lal Seth was beside himself. With nothing more to lose, he prepared for a final assault. Hurling curses at the top of his voice, he rushed out of his haveli, firing randomly at the mob from his .303 rifle. The crowd stood still for a moment as two of their comrades fell to the bullets, and then they charged at Rai Bahadur, bludgeoning him to death. Ironically, the attack was led by Rai Bahadur's barber. Within minutes, five of the family were dead and their home destroyed by a mob that continued to chant slogans, carrying plundered loot in one hand and blood on the other.

Sham Sunder and Roshini were not at home. They were at Jata Jamaalpur near Lahore to see off Roshini's brother Baldev Raj Chopra. Baldev had a shop called Lala Kedar Nath & Sons. It was the shop from where he ran his cloth business. He had decided to close both his shop and house and was leaving for Amritsar the next day with his family. He planned on staying away till the agitation subsided and peace was once again restored in the region. He had dug a hole under the mango tree in his courtyard and had hidden the family's valuables in it. They were to carry only a few hundred rupees with them— he did not think they would need more as it would probably not be very long before they were back. Sham Sunder, who had earlier told his brother-in-law that there was no need to panic and that normalcy would be restored soon, now had a change of heart. He thought it was a wise idea to go across the border for a while and decided that as soon as he returned to Lahore the next day, he would speak to his father and sisters and begin their move to Amritsar as well. However, things were going to be very different. Within a couple of hours of the incident, Sham Sunder heard of the death of his father and sisters. He broke down. He screamed and wept uncontrollably. He could not understand why the police or the military had not intervened and saved the victims. Later in the evening Sham Sunder gathered courage and strength and, after assimilating the enormity and seriousness of the situation, decided to leave for Amritsar with Baldev. There was no going back! The next morning, Sham Sunder and Baldev left with their families to board the train to Amritsar.

During that time, there were instances of trains being ambushed. Those going to Amritsar and Delhi from Sialkot, Rawalpindi, Peshawar and Lahore were stopped midway and the occupants butchered to death, leaving a bloody trail with many injured. The same had happened with some of those coming from Delhi, Calcutta and Amritsar towards Lahore. They had met the same fate on the other side of the newly-drawn border between India and Pakistan. However, people who wished to get away were still taking the chance. Only, the situation kept deteriorating by the day.

At the station in Lahore, and to their dismay, Sham Sunder and Baldev found the train to Amritsar overflowing with people; even the roof was full of people. Everyone was in a rush to get to safety across the border. Sham Sunder and Baldev tried to get their wives and children into the ladies' cabin of a compartment but it was crammed to full capacity. They enquired about the schedule of the next departure and were told that there were not many chances of another train leaving that day.

Dark smoke began to rise from buildings in the vicinity of the station and an uproar rent the air. Houses of Hindus that lay in the vicinity were being gutted. Just then a large throng of assailants brandishing swords came charging on to the platform. The driver hurriedly sprang into action and started the engine of the train. There was a sudden jerk and the train lurched forward. The crowd of passengers on the platform went berserk and made a dash to get it. A small contingent of police tried to control the assailants but it was all in vain, for the mob was obsessed with settling scores. Sham Sunder somehow managed to push his wife and son into a compartment. Seeing Baldev struggling to board his family through the second door of the compartment, Sham Sunder ran to help, and because the train had begun to pick up speed, he got in after them. The train gathered momentum and Sham Sunder heaved a sigh of relief— all of them were on board. But fifteen kilometres short of the border, there was a surprise attack. It was what everyone had feared. At first, gun shots sounded in the distance, and then those shots became louder along with the neighing of horses and shouts of distress. Suddenly, the train halted and the sound of indiscriminate firing and cries began to fill the air. The people on the roof fell first. In minutes, hundreds of them had fallen to bullets, like skittles.

There were many such as Baldev and his family who jumped off the train and hurtled themselves across the fields in a bid to escape. But a large number were gunned down. Innocent passengers were fired at or struck down with swords and daggers. Finally, the mayhem stopped and it was over. There was no movement except for the rustle of the breeze as it blew across the vegetation that was now wet in pools of red blood. The fanatics left the train with hundreds of dead bodies scattered across its floors. It was their compliments to those across the border. Revenge had been taken and justice meted out to their brethren killed in a similar manner on the other side.

Sham Sunder lay still, hardly daring to breathe. His head hurt where he had fallen. The man standing next to him had been riddled with bullets, and as the latter fell, he had taken him down too. Covered in the man's blood, Sham Sunder had lain still, pretending to be dead and so he had managed to escape the killers. The voices of the other survivors now filled the air. People called out to each other, some wailed in pain, names could be heard, and the foul stench of blood and death spread across the ill-fated train to Wagah. Sham Sunder's first thought was that of Roshini and Rahul. Pushing away the limp body lying on top of him, he got down from the train. He had to step over a sea of bloody corpses to get into the compartment where he had left Roshni and Rahul; but his wife and son were nowhere to be seen. Frantically, he searched the entire compartment; he even looked for them in the fields across which bodies lay strewn. He called for them, but they were not to be found. Sham Sunder cried in anguish. He could not imagine what could have happened. Where had they gone? All he could do was pray that his wife and son had somehow escaped amongst those who had crossed the fields.

The survivors discussed their course of action. Hundreds lay dead and an equal number lay injured who needed immediate medical attention. They would have to get the train across the border to safety. Accompanied by two other men, Sham Sunder went to the engine where he found the driver severely wounded and the two helpers dead. Taking instructions from the driver, he started the engine himself. Sham Sunder had never in his life faced such a precarious situation. He, along with the other men, shovelled coal into the furnace, and there was a sense of shared relief as the train moved forward and picked up speed. The work helped keep his mind off his family, and though he feared the worst, the feeling was numbed as he fed coal after more coal. The men kept the engine going—their only thought being to get the train safely across the border to its destination. The train finally arrived at Attari Station at Wagah Border where all hell broke loose. People waiting to receive their brethren, as well as others who had collected to see for themselves what had become of the train, raised a collective cry as it came to a halt on the platform. The British Company commander in charge of the Gurkha contingent took control of the situation with great difficulty. Sham Sunder looked for his family one more time. He checked across the length of the train, but finally he had to give up.

The events had been narrated to me by my father several times, and many times I had dreamt of my mother in the same salwar kameez and green zari dupatta she had worn in the photograph.

Kheer Bhawani Temple was situated approximately forty kilometers from Srinagar, a little ahead of Daichi Gram Resort. I was intrigued; why on earth had Ayesha Begum chosen to live in a Hindu temple? As we arrived there, I first offered my prayers before the idol of Goddess Kheer Bhawani. I was both anxious and optimistic and I wished for divine grace on my side.

I prayed with all my heart for blessings so that the meeting I was going to have would be a fruitful one. As I rose from my kneeling position, my eyes fell on an elderly lady in a white saree coming towards the temple. She walked with some difficulty, and as she slowly made her way to the shrine something about her struck me. There was something very familiar about her. It was the photograph! She was much older now, but I recognized the facial features that were a true copy of the picture I had been holding dear all these years. It was no wonder she was staying at a Hindu temple. She was not Ayesha Begum but Roshini Seth—my lost mother! She reached the shrine and I bent before my goddess, my heart thudding and my brain became numb. With folded hands and tears in my eyes, I touched her feet. She looked at me in bewilderment for a few seconds, and then suddenly, for some inexplicable reason, tears sparkled in her eyes and she murmured, 'Rahul! Is it you?'

No words were exchanged between the mother and son who were meeting after fifty-three years, but tears flowed and emotions poured out. She held me for a long time, and then I made my way to a telephone booth and called my father in Mumbai. There was a long silence before he could find his voice. He was choking...he could not believe it...he asked to speak to her. It was a long while before my parents disconnected the phone on either side of the line. They had barely spoken to each other, absolutely overwhelmed by the happenings. My mother was relieved to hear that her brother Baldev and his family had survived the massacre on the train, and she spoke to him on telephone too. She told him how his friend Virpal Singh had helped her at the Lahore railway station, and that it was only because of him that she and Rahul were alive. But Virpal had not survived, her brother told her. Mother was taken aback; she looked at me questioningly. I wondered who Virpal was but knew I would have to wait till mother told us her story.

She was now calm and looked composed. Apart from the arthritis that ailed her, she had done well with regard to her physical health, perhaps because of her disciplined life at the ashram. She followed her daily routine of prayers, meditation and duties at the temple, and these had given her the fortitude to carry on. My father took the first flight to Srinagar the next morning. It was a tearful reunion—one that we had longed for ever since I could remember.

The other residents of the temple and the adjoining ashram where my mother lived were amazed to hear the story of Ayesha Begum. She had never revealed it to them. They recollected how, initially, they had been a little wary of her presence amongst them, but they had soon taken to her and had begun regarding her as a pious lady who looked after the clothing of the idols in the temple. She was well respected and came to be referred to as 'Ammaji'. After Usman Ali's sisters were married and their mother had died, she had had no purpose in continuing to live in their house. She had come to the ashram to devote her life to her prayers and had made it her home.

It was time to go back to her own home. A large number of people emerged from the temple complex to see us off and bid farewell to Ammaji. Before leaving, I went back into the temple shrine and prostrated myself at the feet of the goddess. The cup of my life had just been filled to the brim; there was nothing more I could ask for. My heart was grateful.

Back in Srinagar, as all of us sat sipping tea in the beautiful garden of Suhail's bungalow, my mother told us that she had visited Amritsar and Delhi a number of times, along with Salma to look for us, but she had only been disappointed each time. She remembered visiting New Delhi in the last week of May 1964, when the first prime minister of independent India, Jawaharlal Nehru, had passed away. She had stood along with the crowd outside Indian Coffee House at Connaught Place to watch the funeral procession as it went past, when she thought she caught a glimpse of her husband in the large gathering present there. Afterwards, she had rushed to the spot on the other side of the road but could not find him. My father intervened to say that he was indeed present on that occasion in Connaught Place. He had stood at the very spot she mentioned. They had been so close!

No, she had not been on board the train to Wagah that ill-fated day! Sham Sunder had forced her in, but there being no space, she had been pushed out and literally thrown on the platform in the surge of the overzealous crowd. She had suffered a broken leg but managed to save her child. She had watched as Sham Sunder climbed in at the other entrance but it was too late! In the noise of all the confusion, her calling out to him was not heard. As the train left the station, Roshini had stared unbelievingly after it. She lay on the platform in that agonizing condition and a terrible fear gripped her as she tightly clutched her child to her chest. She looked around desperately—the thought of saving her child paramount on her mind as she witnessed the shrieks and screams of people falling to the mob that had gone wild. They would not survive was her only thought. Suddenly, a Sikh appeared from nowhere, and supporting her with one arm and the child with the other, he half dragged and half carried Roshini into an inner waiting lounge of the station.

He was Virpal Singh, a close friend of Baldev. He was alarmed at her predicament, and overcome by emotion, he vowed to help her and her child reach the border safely. She was not only his friend's sister but his too, he stated. Roshini was moved to tears and she begged Virpal Singh to take her son with him as she could not move due to her injury. Barely conscious in her pain, she knew she would not be able to save her child. She told him of Baldev's plan to go to relatives in Amritsar; her husband would be there too. If god were with her, she would survive, but at that moment she needed to ensure her son's safety and he was safer with Virpal Singh. Baldev's friend did not wish to leave her in that condition, but her words made sense. So, giving her his blessings, he took the infant in his arms. He told her he would take any vehicle that was leaving Lahore and get to Amritsar. And that was the last she saw of Virpal Singh.

The waiting lounge was occupied mainly with women and children, and outside stood a group of Hindu and Sikh youngsters guarding the entrance. Wielding knives and kirpans, (the short swords carried by Sikhs), as well as wooden sticks and axes, they had positioned themselves and were fighting off the assailants who tried to come closer. Those in the waiting lounge knew they were not going to remain safe for long. The ruthless mob would be upon them soon, for they had no qualms about attacking women and even children.

In the midst of the commotion, Roshini heard someone call her name. It was Salma, her friend from DAV School at Lahore who was now married to Mir Qasim Ali of Srinagar. She had come on a visit to Lahore to meet her father and was returning home. As luck would have it, she had taken refuge in the waiting lounge to save herself from the bedlam on the platform. The two of them held each other, glad to be with a familiar face in that fearful circumstance.

The situation outside began to grow worse. Bodies lay scattered on the platform and there was blood splattered everywhere. The few policemen who had come to control the mob had at first tried to stop the slaughter, but when their own had begun to fall, they fled the scene. Salma grew frightened. She knew her friend's condition would not allow her to even stand up, leave alone save herself, so she did the best thing she could think of. Taking out a burqa—the loose, outer garment worn by women of Muslim countries—she made Roshini wear it, and then she removed her friend's bindi and her mangal sutra—these being marriage symbols of her Hindu religion. It was the only way to save her.

After the carnage was over, only a few Muslim women and men remained at the station. These included Salma and her companion Ayesha Begum—the new name Salma had just given Roshini whom she called her sister. Salma insisted on taking Roshini with her to Srinagar. She could not possibly leave her behind in that condition. Roshini, in her semi-unconscious state, could not protest. Calling for help, Salma had Roshini's leg tended to, and along with her, boarded the evening train to Srinagar. And that is how a new lease of life began for Roshini, or Ayesha Begum with Salma and her family.

After her daughters had been married, Salma suffered suffered poor health for some years. Ayesha Begum took good care of her, for how could she ever forget how her friend had helped her in her hour of need. But when Salma died, she had felt no purpose in living in the same house. She now wished to live the rest of her life in an ashram, and that was when she went to the Kheer Bhawani Temple complex. My father explained how he had heard his name being announced over the loudspeaker at the refugee camp at Amritsar, and when he rushed to the camp commander's office, he had been overjoyed to find Rahul there. The commander had informed him that a very badly injured person had handed over the child to him. There was no mention of the mother. Thereafter, my father had continued to search for my mother. No one could tell what had happened to Virpal Singh. Was he the one who left Rahul at the camp? Did he send the child through someone else as he himself could not make it? We would never know, but in our hearts, we silently prayed silently for his soul.

It was time to let go of the past. I suggested we plan a grand homecoming for my mother who was returning to her family after five decades. We could continue to do all the catching-up afterwards. I, for one, was determined to have her make up for all the affection I had been deprived of for so many years. That night, at Rawalpura House, I slept at my mother's feet like a child.

The Suicide Note

Creators of any genre of writing—be it playwrights, novelists, poets or others—have the choice of writing either fiction or non-fiction. They are guided by the direction in which their hearts beat finding stimulus through their imagination or inspired by happenings in the world around them. They also have another choice—to give the world their name or keep their identity anonymous. Shah Nawaz chose the latter, but whether he did it out of choice or a compulsion is another matter.

Shah Nawaz lived in Badshah Nagar of Lucknow. He was, what could be called, a true novelist. He enjoyed creating long narratives around his imaginary characters and events, and he breathed such quality of life into his work that his stories seemed real. He was a learned writer, having obtained a Masters in English literature from Lucknow University. Much respected by the fraternity as well as the public for his works, Shah Nawaz, over the years, created his own niche as one from the era of the erstwhile Lucknow that was steeped in grace and morality. He not only upheld ethical laws but also became the epitome of virtuous thoughts and deeds. But Shah Nawaz carried a deep scar in his heart, although it was not visible because of the shell he had created around him.

From his childhood days he was known to be a recluse, one who preferred to remain aloof rather than join boys his age as they played in the evenings in the fields near River Gomti. He was an introvert who lived in his own world. His only friends were his books.

He was six years old when his mother passed away and his father remarried. His stepmother turned out to be his worst nightmare. Shafi, the name lovingly given to him by his mother, was tormented by his stepmother. She made him do difficult chores around the haveli in which they lived and would often beat him without reason. She delighted in making him suffer and warned him of dire consequences should he ever complain to his father. For a child at that tender age it was a traumatic experience, one that cut across his raw emotions and scarred him forever. The daily acts of cruelty in the shelter of his own home pushed him into a shell from which he could never totally come out.

His father remained oblivious to his suffering. The stepmother assumed a façade in his presence, acting as though she cared for the boy just to win her husband's approval. He could never imagine what she was up to behind his back.

Shafi had a maternal uncle, Mohammed Sami Ahmed, his deceased mother's brother, who was very fond of him. Ahmed had some inkling of his nephew's plight and sympathized with him, and though he could not openly interfere in the affairs of his brother-in-law's home without causing further distress for his nephew, he imparted to Shafi a dictum that helped the boy cope with his life. He told him to 'speak for one hour, meditate for two hours and walk for four hours every day to maintain the balance of life'. Shafi began following this maxim sincerely and it helped him face his situation. He looked forward to the times he spent with his uncle as he came to depend on him for strength. But there was another reason too. His uncle's daughter, Fatima, brought fragrance to Shafi's life and he grew to be very fond of her. He laughed a lot in her company and learnt to open his heart to her. At other times Shafi poured his heart out in his diary. It was his little secret companion when he was alone. He gave vent to his emotions through his writings in it, and this made him feel lighter. He also began to write about other things and soon developed a keen interest in painting his visual images through his words.

He was twelve when his father died and he was left entirely at the mercy of his stepmother. The next six years were extremely difficult. He never gathered the courage to confront her, though he himself was a growing boy, and so his ordeal continued. It only ended with her demise. Shah Nawaz, now a young adult, had by this time developed a deep love for Fatima. He was sure he wanted to spend the rest of his life with her. She was indeed beautiful. Her deep, lucid eyes and long, flowy black hair stirred the writer in him. They would meet secretly and he would share his writings with her, these being mostly romantic couplets written in praise of her charm. She would be genuinely impressed with the eloquent lines of Shah Nawaz and the manner in which he articulated himself. There, on the terrace of her house, under the myriad stars in the sky, they would fill each other's hearts with love. Shah Nawaz wanted to marry Fatima with all his heart, but he lacked the courage to express his desire to his uncle who, however, had understood that the two had feelings for each other. It was he who broached the topic, and one bright morning he called the family maulvi and had their nikah performed. Shah Nawaz, at twenty years, was thus united with Fatima in marriage, and days of happiness commenced for him.

Those who interacted with him often—his friends and relatives—liked Shah Nawaz for his calm and composed demeanour. Little did they know of the wounds he carried deep in his heart. He had taught himself the virtue of quietude and now, blessed with his new life with the person he desired, he was actually happy. His wife took good care of him and for the first time in his life after losing his mother he felt truly loved. He almost forgot the misery he had been through.

Shah Nawaz joined The Convent School where he taught English literature. He drew a nominal salary. He and Fatima could not afford to indulge in the luxuries of life, yet they were contented. They lived in a world of their own. Time passed and just as one is faced with the harsh realities that come along the journey of life, this couple had to face their challenges too. Five years had gone by without an offspring. A thorough medical check-up revealed that Fatima could not conceive. Shah Nawaz felt wretched. He accepted it as god's will and tried to come to terms with it, however, it started affecting their relationship. Small quarrels and clashes ensued and became bigger ones. Fatima's father, a wise man, understood the reason for the rift between his daughter and son-in-law and, faced with the truth, he knew there was only one solution—that his son-in-law get married again.

Both Mohammed Sami Ahmed and Fatima now insisted for the remarriage. She assured Shah Nawaz that once there were children in the home, it would benefit their own relationship. It would all be beautiful once again. With great reluctance, Shah Nawaz married for the second time. Sheena Malik, his new wife, belonged to Lucknow. He had four children from her—one son and three daughters, including twin girls. Two wives and four children lived with Shah Nawaz in his old haveli. In public view, Fatima and Sheena appeared to get along well with each other, but it was all a pretence. Within the walls of the house there were periodic outbursts between them. Fatima, the older and wiser of the two, exhibited more patience, but when Sheena got aggressive she retaliated as well and quarrels followed. The two wives began to despise each other, and as the years went by and the children grew older, Shah Nawaz just about managed to keep his family together under the same roof.

Shah Nawaz's first passion had always been his writing. Although his school employment was a duty that he performed diligently and it brought in his salary at the end of the month, his heart lay in his stories. He spent as much time as possible writing them. When he was forty-eight he finally took the plunge and left his school employment for full-time writing. Apart from novels he tried his hand at genres like drama, lyrics and poetry. But due to the prevailing economic conditions, times were tough. The price index had risen sharply. His means were limited and Shah Nawaz found it difficult to run his home and pay for the education and other expenses of his children. He also had two wives to take care of.

Around this time Shah Nawaz's eldest daughter Ruhina married Salman, a small-time automobile mechanic at a workshop in Aminabad. Shah Nawaz had been against the idea of his daughter's alliance with an illiterate man whom he had disliked from their very first meeting, but on Sheena's insistence he had given in to Ruhina's plea. Soon after the wedding Salman's demands for monetary help began. He wanted to set up his own workshop and also buy a new one-bedroom house to move into with his wife. He asked for support for both. Salman's intentions were not honourable and everyone understood that his eyes were on the ancestral haveli of his father-in-law. To Shah Nawaz, who was already struggling financially, these demands added further anxiety to his state of mind.

The times were certainly challenging for Shah Nawaz. A conventional and staunch believer in the old school of thought, whose writings reflected his views on social and moral issues that plagued society, Shah Nawaz had enjoyed the appreciation of his readers. But lately he found, to his dismay, his fan-following slowly shrinking. People's preferences in the fields of literature and reading were changing, and this trend was noticed even with the popular mushairas held in Lucknow that once received endless applause. A poetry recital no longer drew the kind of crowd it used to. It was not the same anymore. The modern generation wanted fast-paced crime thrillers and romantic novels. Publishers, too, looked for authors who could compose with the new demand in sight, and writers such as Shah Nawaz began to suffer. His savings dwindled rapidly. Shah Nawaz was perturbed. The paucity of funds at home resulted in embarrassment for the family. His children faced reminders from their school and college for fee payment, and the squabbles between his wives, under the existing tension in the house, remained no longer hidden. Hard-pressed for money, he was beside himself with anxiety.

Shah Nawaz knew he had to find a way to increase his income. He was a good man, disciplined and devoted to his religion. He took care of his health and was extremely particular about his morning walk in the neighbourhood park. With health and wellbeing on his side, he looked forward to years of work to sustain himself. He approached his school friend Mukesh Mathur, editor with Nawab Publications. The latter voiced his concern. Shah Nawaz would have to change his style of writing, he said. Being the practical man he was, even though it went against his ethical standards, Shah Nawaz agreed to write a book that would lure readers. He needed the money to take care of his family.

He wrote a novel on crime, sex and violence, and created suspense, thrills, twists and turns—in complete contrast to his own principles and paradigms. If that was what the market wanted, so be it! But he chose to keep it a secret; he did not wish his name associated with something that was not his truth. He wrote under the pseudonym 'Dilip Kumar' in the style of the legendary film actor whom he idolized. Nawab Publications printed three thousand copies of the thriller. Shah Nawaz earned a neat two-and-a-half lakh rupees from his new work. The initial copies were sold in no time and Mukesh Mathur, on receiving a positive response from booksellers, printed another three thousand copies. He promised Shah Nawaz a hefty royalty from further sales. Shah Nawaz was ecstatic. He could not believe his luck! He had become rich overnight. In the face of success, traces of conventional thinking and dos and don'ts that he still held in his mind were wiped off once and for all. He bought gifts for his family and on Eid, the family celebrated the festival after a long time.

He did not reveal the work or his pen name to anyone, for he had written something that was not in line with his self-image. He stashed the money away, deciding not to let his family know of it. He did not want them to think there was plenty and indulge themselves without thought. He did, however, present copies of his book to his wives and friends who read it with interest. They even liked it. Shah Nawaz stared incredulously after them. He could not believe it! He failed to comprehend their keenness for a novel that was, according to him, bereft of any social message, intelligence or significance. But it was a moment of awakening for him. And now that he had money, Shah Nawaz thought of writing another novel.

He had planned on talking to Mukesh Mathur for another project when he had a chance meeting with a television serial producer, Akash Seth, at The Coffee House. It was 1997. Multiple television channels had emerged by this time and these vied for viewership through the variety of programmes they offered. Producers were constantly on the lookout for interesting stories they could adapt as scripts. Akash was in the process of finalizing plans for his forthcoming serial *Dahej* that was based on the issue of dowry. He needed the screenplay as soon as possible and he asked Shah Nawaz to write it for him without delay. The theme was of interest to the writer. It reflected a malaise in communities and families where a custom was taken advantage of and distorted by many to the extent of their greed. He accepted the assignment.

Shah Nawaz his enquiries on the subject as he always did in preparation for his writings. For most of his research work he frequented various libraries in the city, and for his current topic he also spoke to families that he knew were facing dowry issues, where sons-in-law had only one source of income—their in-laws. Shah Nawaz looked forward to writing the script but he was continuously distracted by the bickering between the two women in his house. He had failed to bring peace between them and preferred to look for an alternative solution, that is, remove himself from the scene so he could peacefully engage himself in his work. He found the answer to his predicament in a secluded corner encircled by trees at the end of a long park, a short distance from his home. Not many visitors came to this patch of the park and it was here that he felt he could immerse himself in his writing for long stretches of time without being disturbed. He began to spend time at this place daily, and found himself enjoying his seclusion and productivity in the midst of natural surroundings.

One late afternoon Shah Nawaz left for his designated spot, carrying his work bag with him. The winter sun warmed him, and he was cheerful for he had been able to maintain a steady flow of work. Being on schedule brought a sense of satisfaction to him. He was nearing the end of the story and was to write the most important scene of the final episode of the script—the climax. Having conceptualized it, he looked forward to putting it into words, and he had informed Fatima of a possible delay in return in the evening as he wanted to finish the section in one go. Arriving at his corner of the park he made himself comfortable, and taking out a writing pad from his bag he began to write.

The story, as he had been instructed to develop, revolved around the lives of a family, mainly the father and daughter vis-à-vis the evils of the dowry system. The girl, after her marriage, is caught in the mire of a husband and his family who treat her as their golden goose; and when she cannot meet their demands, they mistreat her. The father is caught between the demands of his daughter's in-laws on the one hand and the miseries of his personal life with a consistently quarrelsome wife on the other. Ultimately, fed up with life's challenges, he decides to end it all. And just before he does so, he writes a note that constitutes the climax of the serial—the note that Shah Nawaz now mulled over and wrote with fervour. It went like this:

'I am tired of the daily quarrels that I am subjected to with my wife. She has no respect for me. She is suspicious by nature and thinks I do not care for her or the children. She does not conduct herself well and uses foul language. She wants me to give in to the repeated dowry demands of my son-in-law who wants to establish his own business and keeps asking me for financial assistance. She does not understand or support me when I tell her that we need to save money to get our other children educated and married. She accuses me of having hidden my mother's jewellery, and when I tell her there is nothing, she does not believe me. She thinks I do not want to give it to her. I cannot deal with my financial difficulties any longer nor can I bear the torture and humiliation I have to go through every day in my own house. I am tired of my life and have decided to end it. I hold my wife responsible for making my life miserable and for driving

me to commit this final act of my life.'

Shah Nawaz had started feeling uneasy. His face flushed and his breathing became difficult. Somehow, he finished writing his script. Maybe it was the midday sun or he had been concentrating too much. There should be no cause for worry, he told himself; his health was good. But the restlessness increased. There were spasms and an acute pain lifted from his left arm. He tried to shout for help, but the pain became unbearable. He gasped for breath as his body started to perspire. Then, suddenly, his heart ceased to beat. He fell to the ground, and his limp body rolled sideways, face down. It was hours before the lifeless Shah Nawaz was discovered in the corner of the park. A gardener alerted his supervisor who immediately summoned an ambulance and rushed the body to L.D. Hospital at University Road.

The chief medical officer of the hospital, as per law, informed the police of the unknown person 'brought dead' and handed over the belongings found along with the body: a water bottle and a bag that contained various items—a wallet with a hundred and forty rupees, a pair of spectacles, a watch, a handkerchief, a writing pad and a pen.

The SHO of the area, a stout man with a big, pointed moustache that he habitually twirled, registered a case against unknown persons under section 406 of the Indian Penal Code that deals with 'abetment to suicide'. It is a punishable offence, if proven guilty, with upto seven years of imprisonment. The SHO took custody of the body and sent it for a post-mortem examination to a government hospital in Hazartganj.

Back in the haveli the wives of Shah Nawaz were worried.

It was now 7.00 p.m. and beyond the time limit the husband had given. Fatima sought the help of their neighbour Salim to look for him. It was dark and Salim, realizing the difficulty for the women to be out, hurriedly left to make enquiries. It did not take him long to trace the events. At the park the watchman on evening duty informed him of an unknown person having been found there earlier who was rushed to the L.D. Hospital at University Road. Salim went to the hospital where, to his shock, he learnt of Shah Nawaz's death. He was also informed that the body had been sent for a post-mortem, and for any further assistance he would have to approach the police. Enquiries at the police station did not reveal much. It wore a deserted look on that late winter evening, and the three policemen on duty, who were chewing tobacco and chatting in front of a fire in the courtyard, did not show any interest. All they could say was that the SHO was out and would be returning shortly. Salim waited. About forty-five minutes later, the SHO arrived and things stirred up. The three policemen got back on their feet and hovered around trying to appear useful.

SHO Karim Khan was aware that the autopsy report would come in after two days, but he was not waiting for it. He had his hands on the most important evidence he needed—the 'suicide note' written by the deceased person prior to his death. It was on the first page of the writing pad found as a part of the belongings of Shah Nawaz and Khan believed it was enough proof to nail the perpetrators of the suicide. When Salim met him, Khan recorded his statement that he was compelled to give—that Shah Nawaz had not been earning well and there were frequent quarrels in the house. Khan showed him the note. Salim was shaken. He recognized and confirmed that the contents of the note were in Shah Nawaz's handwriting. The wily SHO smiled. He now had further confirmation to support his conclusion.

News of the death spread like wildfire across the neighbourhood of the residence of the deceased. All those who had known him—relatives, friends, acquaintances—reacted with shock and disbelief. It was impossible! And when they heard it was a case of suicide and that a note had been found with the body, it was the horror of horrors. The wives could not accept it. The circumstances had never been that extreme for him to have taken such a drastic step, so they believed.

Karim Khan visited the neighbourhood to look for further information. The residents, acquainted with the SHO's overbearing attitude eyed him coldly as he stomped about throwing questions, mostly irrelevant, related to the family of the writer and their behaviour towards their neighbours. Khan was working on his own assumptions and the investigation was a mere formality—he had already arrived at his conclusion. The family of Shah Nawaz stood silent, bewildered by what had happened. Ruhina stood with them, crying bitterly. Her husband had not accompanied her. Fatima and Sheena held the children together and sniffed into their dupattas, tears trickling down their cheeks. They looked a pitiable lot as neighbours tried to console them, but Khan was not moved in the least. The SHO showed little regard for the two widows. He had seen many a drama being enacted in front of his eyes to be concerned about the sorrow of the weeping wives. He was convinced beyond any doubt after reading the suicide note that it was a case of abetment to suicide—a punishable crime—and the wives were guilty of it. They were the root cause of the extreme step taken by their husband and Karim Khan vowed to penalize them. The ladies were perplexed and could not answer his unwarranted questions and nor could the neighbours.

Salim lost his patience, and backed by other neighbours he suggested that the SHO stick to the point and ask relevant questions. Raising his voice he accused Khan of causing the family unnecessary distress. Karim Khan flew into a rage and slapped him. He asked his subordinates to book charges against him for obstructing the work of government officials on duty. He had done nothing of the sort, but he knew that the SHO meant business and had the power to put him behind bars. The SHO now threatened all those present of terrible consequences, using third degree methods, if they did not cooperate and reveal details as he asked because abetment to suicide was a serious offence and so was obstructing an official on duty. He then pressed charges against both Fatima and Sheena and, with the support of lady constables, took them along with him for questioning. There was chaos at the police station. Relatives and friends of the family began to gather there after hearing the news. Fatima pleaded before Khan that Shah Nawaz was not the kind of person to commit suicide. If he had intended it, he would have behaved in a different manner that afternoon before leaving home. She told the SHO that Shah Nawaz had in fact seemed cheerful. If he had any intention of not returning home again he would have entered his children's room for a last look at them, but he did not do that. His committing suicide did not appeal to reason at all.

But Karim Khan was not convinced. He told them he would ensure they were not granted bail and remained behind bars for at least six months. He had by now got wind of the fact that Salman had been asking for money on a regular basis. It validated the contents of the note left by Shah Nawaz.

All of a sudden it struck Fatima that her husband had mentioned something about writing a script for Akash Seth, the television producer. She asked a relative of hers to contact the latter immediately; maybe he would be able to throw some light on the matter.

Luckily, Zeeshan Ali walked in on the scene. He was a close relative of the SHO, a neighbour of the family, and he had always had great respect for Shah Nawaz. He had heard of the news and decided to interven. Taking the SHO aside, he requested him to wait for the results of the post-mortem examination before registering an FIR, because once an FIR was registered the family would unnecessarily be drawn into an unending legal battle. Khan did not think it was unnecessary but he slyly suggested to Ali that he talk to the family and ask them to come forward for a settlement. Ali understood what he meant; Khan was openly asking for a bribe to quash the matter. He took the wives outside and conveyed what Khan wanted. They had no money but agreed to arrange for one lakh rupees. But Khan wanted five lakhs in order to not press charges against them and wait for the post-mortem report. Zeeshan Ali shuttled between the two parties, negotiating for them, till he finally helped them arrive at a settlement. It was decided that Fatima and Sheena would arrange for a sum of three lakh rupees in exchange for Shah Nawaz's note. All the while Khan behaved as though it were a routine matter for him. He now addressed Fatima and Sheena, his stance completely changed. The tough bearing had suddenly melted into a softer one. He said out loud, so everyone could hear, that he would wait for the post-mortem report before further action. The wives could return home till then. He kept the note in his pocket. It was a precious promissory note that would be yielding him income.

The crowd left leaving behind a smiling Khan. He was proud of the manner in which he had created pressure on them. It was an opportunity he was not going to let pass so easily. He then opened his table drawer, drew some flavoured tobacco out of a sachet, and grinning to himself put it in his mouth, revealing his charcoal-coloured teeth.

People once again gathered in the open courtyard of the house of Fatima and Sheena. Though it was night time, they did not want to leave. No one could sleep. They discussed the reason for the death of their dear Shah Nawaz and tried to make sense of the suicide note. How could he have written it and why would he have done so? It mentioned the quarrel with the wife, the demands of the son-in-law, and the responsibility of the other children. To those who did not know Shah Nawaz well enough it would seem he wrote it, because it was similar to his prevailing circumstances. But for those who knew him well a huge question mark remained as to why he would write such a note.

While the discussion was going on Fatima's relative walked in along with Akash Seth and Mukesh Mathur. They had been told of the mysterious circumstance of the death and the suicide note that was found. Akash immediately put the puzzle pieces together. The note, he said, had undeniably been written by Shah Nawaz but it was for another purpose—it happened to be part of the script he was working on for Akash's forthcoming serial. Mukesh Mathur spoke and praised Shah Nawaz's earlier work, revealing to them that the writer had been paid a substantial sum of money for it. The widows stared at him in surprise for Shah Nawaz had never disclosed it to them.

Fatima and Sheena hurried inside to check their husband's belongings and storage spaces. Neatly concealed in an envelope, in a corner of a drawer in his wardrobe, they found two lakh fifteen thousand rupees in currency notes. Now the question was would they still need to settle with Khan? Ali believed it would not be necessary since the reason for the existence of the note had been revealed. He requested Akash to accompany them to inform the SHO about the script Shah Nawaz had been writing.

The next morning, Zeeshan Ali, Salim and Akash Seth met the SHO once again. Akash apprised Khan about the truth behind the note and the details of his serial that Shah Nawaz had been writing the script for. He also told him about the novel written by Shah Nawaz under a pseudonym for Nawab Publications. The SHO stared at them for a moment as though deliberating the issue, and then he assumed a tough stance once again. No, he was in no mood to listen to them. He was adamant on the theory of the suicide note since it reflected the life of the deceased. He accused Akash Seth, instead, of fabricating another story and trying to write a fresh script to cover the truth. Khan kept blabbering ruthlessly, saying he would have the son-in-law Salman brought in for questioning, and also that he would be forced to register the case and arrest the culprits if they did not 'settle' the matter at once.

Extremely disappointed with the outcome, Ali, Salim and Akash returned to Fatima and Sheena. They sat down once again to discuss the problem. By the afternoon, they were able to come to a decision. There was only one thing to do. Taking two lakhs from the widows of Shah Nawaz, they went to Akash's office first and then to meet the SHO.

They gave him the money with the promise to pay the balance one lakh rupees at the earliest. Karim Khan thanked his stars that his plan had worked. He was glad he had taken the opportunity to make some extra income, which he often made using such blackmail tactics. He handed them Shah Nawaz's written note and agreed to wait till the post-mortem report was ready. Karim Khan later counted the money, his fingers moving faster than ever. He imagined showering them on Munni Bai Jaan, his mistress.

The three men smiled as they left the police station for the second time that day. Later in the evening, when they called and left a message for the SHO to watch a certain news channel, the obstinate Karim Khan faced the biggest shock of his life. He was on prime time television, accepting bribe in a sting operation. It had been captured discreetly by Akash and was now in view of the entire nation. Khan realized the blunder he had committed by threatening a person from the media. He had put his foot in his mouth. Karim Khan was arrested under the Prevention of Corruption Act and booked for taking bribe. The Hon'ble Court refused to even grant him bail and with handcuffs on his wrists, he was entrusted behind the bars as a criminal. His arrogance and bloated ego was crushed.

Two days later, the post-mortem report came in. It stated the cause of death. Shah Nawaz had died of a cardiac arrest and there was no foul play at all. The police case was closed holding that the 'suicide note' had indeed been a part and parcel of the script of the Television Serial. The ordeal of the family members ended and they alongwith others gave a decent burial to the writer Shah Nawaz, alias 'Dilip Kumar'.

King Cobra

Akhil Khanna did exceptionally well in his business management course at the Indian Institute of Management (IIM) in Bengaluru and was offered a monthly package of two-and-a-half lakh rupees along with perquisites by Microsoft India. Akhil was one of those individuals who was both intelligent as well as industrious, and these qualities had made him an excellent student. His father, an IAS officer, was proud of his son's achievement and suggested that he accept the offer from Microsoft. But Akhil had other plans in mind.

Akhil had his eyes on Rohit Jain, two years his senior at IIM, who had opened two restaurants in the posh colonies of Bangalore. Both the places were doing well and drew huge crowds. Akhil admired him and, following his senior's example, he too decided to open his own chain of pub-cum-restaurants in Bangalore and other cities, but with an entirely different concept. Akhil thought out unusual ideas. He wanted one that was a radical shift from the regular monotonous ones on offer in the city; one that bordered on the bizarre. He was bored of conventional and predictable restaurants that offered a similar staid décor and an outdated, run-of-the-mill menu, where one had the feeling of 'if you've visited one, you've visited them all'. He strongly believed that there had to be some exclusivity in making a visit to a restaurant more interesting. The world had closed in and the old school of thought was a thing of the past. People now travelled overseas, they were exposed to various cultures, and they were demanding customers. Moreover, the current younger generation was not only earning well but also spending on entertainment. Their paradigm had changed—they worked hard and partied harder. And they constantly demanded something 'different'. He decided that if they wanted something different then he would give them that.

He finally thought of a concept—it was not just unique, it was shockingly different. The likes of it had never been seen in Bangalore or in any other Indian city he had visited. Akhil shared his idea with his friends from IIM, Pranay Sharma and Omar Shahid, who were immediately fascinated by the project and wanted to be part of it. The three pooled in money and rented a space ad measuring 4000 sq ft on Ulsoor Road. They called it 'The Lizardo', and exactly as its name sounded, it was based on the hair-raising and spine-tingling concept of reptiles! The idea was to attract young people to the pub and give them a touch of the 'creepy and crawly'.

The décor matched the name. Stuffed replicas and artificial skins of lizards, snakes, alligators and crocodiles of various sizes and species crept up on the corners and walls. The grey-green and wood colour palette matched with natural foliage and walls carrying pictures from snake films of the likes of *Anaconda*, *Python* and *Snake Island*. The effect was raw and horrifying, yet the ambience was thrilling! A licence to run it was obtained from government authorities and the pub-cum-restaurant was opened to the public on 26 August. It was Pranay's birthday—the first of their birthdays that came.

The restaurant became a rage and the 'most happening place in town' overnight. The menu was a hit with the young crowd and they loved the feel of the place. The three partners knew the pulse of their customers. They were aware that to reach the top in this line of business, they would have to develop entertaining patterns and have regular gigs and shows. They chose exclusive performers who understood the audience and had the ability to deliver to different demands. The restaurant remained open till the wee hours of the morning, and the crowd poured in throughout the night. On most evenings famous bands played music and delighted the youngsters who ate, drank and danced to their heart's content. The Lizardo became famous and its footfall increased by the day. Aside from word-of-mouth publicity, advertisements in social media proved a boon. The restaurant was rated as the most 'rocking' place in the city on Facebook.

By the end of one year, the sales touched an all-time high of twenty lakh rupees per week. The three friends now inducted a fourth person, Samarjit Singh, as a financier, who invested a large sum to be utilized in the opening up of two more restaurants under the same brand, both in Bangalore. They worked hard and met every Saturday to frame new strategies and introspect. The monthly income statements put before them by the chief financial officers of the three restaurants were also checked. The three pub-cum-restaurants were doing roaring business and the four partners were minting money. It was a success story for them. Their unique concept had hit bulls eye! Akhil had even managed to surpass his idol, Rohit Jain.

Akhil became rich and famous within a span of two years and marriage proposals began to pour in. He decided it was time to settle down. He got married to Ananya, and the wedding ceremony was held at Hotel Taj Malabar at Cochin in Kerala. It was a lavish 'destination wedding' attended by almost six hundred guests. For his honeymoon he had decided to visit Penang, Malaysia. He was charmed by the sea side resort, also called Pulau Pinang, located off the northwest coast of Peninsular Malaysia. He had booked a suite well in advance in a hotel in Tanjung Tokong—a suburb of Georgetown, the capital of Penang. Penang was a picturesque place and mesmerizing to say the least. Their hotel was a wonderful property with a large swimming pool amid artistic landscaping in close proximity to the beach. The honeymoon couple swam, ate heartily at the multi-cuisine restaurants and visited the city centre at Georgetown for shopping. Akhil and Ananya had a memorable time and made the most of their stay in Penang. On the last day, while visiting Georgetown, Akhil's eyes fell on various living and dead reptiles, including a four-metre-long dead king cobra, displayed in a restaurant on Lorong Baru Street. Immediately an idea struck him. He would buy it and display it at his restaurant. He loved the thought of the effect it would have effect on people.

He bought the snake along with its big glass container and brought it to Bangalore, covered in special packaging. He proudly put it on a prominent place of display in The Lizardo, adding yet another creepy crawly to his possessions. The young crowd was captivated. The dangerous king cobra, a rare species and the world's longest venomous snake, looked alive and ready to attack.

Shortly, one more restaurant was opened by Akhil and his partners. Located at Cyber City in Gurgaon, their fourth chain of restaurants was an instant success too. They were on a winning spree, as though blessed with the Midas touch. Akhil's father, who had once discouraged his involvement in the restaurant business, now felt proud of his son's super success.

Years passed and the four partners, who had become thick friends, decided to purchase 94000 sq. ft of land at the village Utorda near Majorda Beach in South Goa. They had, by now, sufficient money to establish and start a hotel on the lines of five-star properties. They had been transferring 25 per cent of their net earnings to a 'project account' which had swelled to a staggering figure of forty-two crore rupees. The remaining amount was to be invested by a consortium of bankers. The latter was keen to support the multimillionaire businessmen who were unstoppable in their endeavours and had sound financial balance sheets.

On a visit to Goa to begin work on the project, the four partners stayed at a South Goa hotel along with their wives. They had several meetings with the architects, interior designers and contractors required for the project. All the while, the sixty-year-old manager of the hotel, Mr Mahendra Kapoor observed them closely. He knew about their stupendous success. One evening, he intentionally sat with them and offered them some elderly advice. He suggested in a fatherly fashion that the four were young and had many years ahead of them. They had great ambitions, but there was no need to overdo things in a bid to achieve their dreams in a hurry. He gave them the example of one of the owners of the hotel they were staying at, who, like them, had been passionate and determined about realizing his goals. He had maintained hectic schedules to establish his hotel business overnight. Being engrossed thus, he had neglected his health, not taken adequate rest and, eventually, had fallen prey to his own ambitions. He had died at a young age due to cardiac failure. Mr Kapoor cautioned them about the repercussions of overindulgence in their work and advised them to go slow so that they did not lose control over their current successful ventures and suffer irreparable losses both financially and health-wise.

The four partners had tasted so much success by this time that they were blinded by their own levels of achievement. They did not pay any heed to the advice as they believed failure could never touch them. Akhil was reminded of his father who had given him a similar warning; but he brushed the thought aside confident that since they had age on their side they could push their bodies for more. Unluckily, and true to the saying, a time of checks and balances struck them without warning.

After a meeting of the foursome that got over at 4.00 a.m., Samarjit decided to go to the gym to stay fit. While on the treadmill he felt giddy but he did not stop. And then he felt severe chest pain and he fell, hurting himself. He was rushed and admitted to Apollo Hospital at Mudgaon in South Goa. He had suffered a heart attack. At thirty-four years of age! By the same afternoon another setback came and Akhil, Shahid and Pranay had to rush back to Bangalore. A raid had taken place on their restaurants by the excise department for violation of laws and to unearth black money allegedly stashed by the multimillionaires.

Akhil and Pranay looked after the legal and financial departments of their organization and everything, from accounts to statutory obligations, was diligently dealt with by them. They were sure nothing was amiss. The excise department also looked for spurious liquor that they had been anonymously informed about. According to an insider, it was being kept and sold in the restaurant. The complainant was perhaps a jealous competitor, someone who was unhappy with the kind of success the four partners had achieved in such a short period of time. For a moment Akhil suspected Rohit Jain being behind the raid and wondered if he could have lodged the complaint.

The officials found nothing incriminating except for a few procedural lapses that had occurred due to the men's overindulgence in the Goa project. There were no spurious liquor nor any infringement of law. But then the officials were intrigued by the dead king cobra and other reptiles displayed in glass jars at The Lizardo. They informed the forest department about the preserved dead reptiles. The forest officer, taking immediate action, arrived with his team, and they confiscated the showpieces from the restaurant. It was only later that Akhil and his partners learnt that the king cobra is considered an 'endangered species' and that it is an offence to display it for commercial purposes or gains.

Akhil admitted to having bought the reptile around seven years ago from a restaurant in Penang. He was asked to produce the documents for its purchase or else he would be booked for killing and displaying an endangered species. Unfortunately, he could not remember the name of the dining place from where he had made the purchase. Neither did he have an invoice or a receipt. And he had not paid through the banking channel, so there was no evidence at all. The forest officer was infuriated.

A case was registered and Akhil was arrested on charges of killing a king cobra and using it for commercial purposes. The statements of Shahid and Pranay were recorded too under section 160 of the Criminal Procedure Code—as it was considered a criminal offence under the Endangered Species Act 1973 and the Wildlife Protection Act 1972. Samarjit was still recuperating at Apollo Hospital in Goa. Akhil was interrogated by the crime branch and sleuths from The Wildlife Crime Control Bureau (WCCB), which later booked him under section 2 of the Wildlife Protection (Amendment) Act 2006 under the heading 'Trophy'. It stated that 'keeping any animal or part thereof was an offence and that using the body parts of an endangered species for commercial purposes was an offence too'.

Akhil was taken to the central jail under judicial custody granted by the court in favour of the WCCB. Akhil simply could not substantiate his claim. Several high-profile lawyers were appointed and representations made before the authorities, but nothing could save him. His father, too, could not help. Akhil's pleas of being innocent fell on deaf ears as they were hellbent on punishing him. His fame and money seemed to have gone against him, for the anti-capitalist bureaucrats of the WCCB made it very clear that they were not going to spare him in spite of his money, influence and connections.

The news of his arrest was splashed all over newspapers and television channels. The restaurants received adverse publicity:

'Tycoon owner of The Lizardo Group arrested for hunting and killing endangered species.' It was spicy news for the media. The habitual young customers at The Lizardo were forbidden by their parents from visiting the reptile-infested restaurant. The reaction from all sides was alarming and the sales at all the four restaurants in Bangalore and Gurgaon dipped for the first time. The partners of Akhil, too, were unable to take control of the restaurant functions, being busy themselves in appointing lawyers to fight the cases registered against them for conspiracy under section 120 B of the Criminal Procedure Code. They were fully absorbed in representing their cases to prove their innocence before the excise and forest departments and the Hon. courts of Bangalore.

The excise and forest department raid was followed by an income tax search and seizure operation on all four restaurants simultaneously. This made matters worse as several documents and papers were seized and the partners were summoned under section 131 of the Income Tax Act 1961.

The police personnel were harsh in their treatment of Akhil, especially for not giving them the answers they wanted to hear. They threatened him of dire consequences if he did not admit to having killed the king cobra. Poor Akhil! He was innocent, so how could he admit to having done such a thing! A charge sheet was filed against him by the WCCB, claiming him to be an offender under the provisions enunciated under sections 2 and 9 of the Wildlife Protection (Amendment) Act 2006.

Luckily, Akhil's lawyers were able to obtain bail for him after proving before the Hon. courts that the king cobra had indeed been brought over from Penang. The glass container holding the reptile had a marking underneath that confirmed it. However, since charges had already been framed against him, it was now up to the courts to follow procedure and give its verdict. Akhil came home after three horrific months, having spent a difficult time in prison with hardcore criminals whom he was no match for. For many days thereafter he remained in a state of depression and became a recluse.

The restaurants had been sealed. The employees had started looking for jobs elsewhere. Akhil, Shahid and Pranay were now completely involved in resolving the income tax, excise and wildlife matters.

There were further setbacks that made the partners feel they were going through a snowball effect. It was found that one of the managers at The Lizardo had been manipulating the accounts by keeping duplicate invoices. These were seized by the income tax authorities on making a thorough search of the premises and resulted in their using the interpolation scheme to enhance the average sales and levy heavy taxes and penalties, for the last seven years, on the organization. Matters thus went from bad to worse and the business was in shambles. But Akhil and his friends exemplified courage. They hung on and did not lose hope in spite of the injustice they faced.

It took several months for Akhil to prove his innocence before the court of law. He was helped by none other than Rohit Jain who, through one of his batch mates from school, was able to trace a receipt with the customs department which clearly indicated that Akhil had paid customs duty on imports made while landing at Bangalore airport seven years ago. Fortunately, he had gone through the red channel and had declared the king cobra in his possession. No customs officer had raised any concern about it. After imposing a duty of thirty-seven thousand rupees the items purchased by him, including the dead reptile, were cleared.

With the passage of time, Akhil slowly recovered from his bouts of depression and Samarjit from his heart ailment. Rohit Jain was a regular visitor to Akhil's house and he helped him get back on his feet again. Akhil was extremely apologetic and he felt guilty for having doubted Rohit. It was Rohit who now advised them to go for a complete makeover—to change the name of their flagship restaurant, The Lizardo, and go for an entirely new theme. The four friends were only too willing. They had had enough of reptiles and vowed never to have anything more to do with endangered species. They had learnt their lesson and suffered enough for it. The restaurant was renamed 'Nautical Miles' and it was refurbished entirely to a more popular and cheerful aqua theme.

Akhil continued to seek the advice of his father and Rohit Jain, who encouraged the partners to face the queries of the three different government departments and sort them out one by one. Akhil's father reminded them using an anecdote: 'Extraordinary people take a problem as a challenge and face it head on while ordinary people consider the same as destiny'. He was a man of wisdom. He told them that they had no reason to remain dejected, for the four of them had a unique quality that could not be taken away from them. It was their shared understanding and affinity that had kept them standing strong and thick in the hour of crisis. Ordinarily, in such a circumstance, partners have been known to have quarrelled and levelled allegations at one another. But they had done nothing of the sort. They had risen above all differences to do with—money, religion, responsibilities and relationships—and had remained true to their partnership and friendship. That was the reason they had survived. They had maintained their trust and unity—the soul of their relationship. There's an old adage, 'Never leave a true relationship for a fault committed by one. Nobody is perfect in this world. Trust, affection and care one day will take one out of the woods'. They had adhered to this adage and proved themselves right.

The four friends had not realized it till then. They had only behaved naturally. Now that Akhil's father had brought it to their notice, it strengthened their belief in their bond. They vowed to restore the business back on its feet. Nautical Miles began to attract customers and the foursome was back in business. They wisely decided to defer the Goa project for now.

The confiscated king cobra was eventually released by the forest department on court orders and Akhil was acquitted of all charges. Ironically, at that moment when he was released, there was no one from the media to cover the event. On the advice of the forest officials Akhil took the dead reptile to an animal cremation ground and had it consigned to flames, putting an end to his ordeal once and for all along with the ashes of the king cobra.

A Misplaced Draft

Anand Prakash Gupta sat on the first floor balcony of his residence, his eyes a little moist but fixed unseeingly on the garden below. It was a sprawling house built on a thousand square yards of land in the upscale locality of Hauz Khas Enclave in New Delhi. Apart from it being a beautiful property, Anand loved the house for many reasons—one of these being the way the garden on the ground floor merged with the adjacent park, giving the impression of a vast green expanse connected to the house.

As he sat there stunned, clutching the Supreme Court orders that had finally given judgement in favour of his nephew, he was unable to fathom that this was to be his last day in this house. The last day! The finality of it hit him hard. He had spent more than forty years of his life here—forty-four long and beautiful years filled with many joyous moments. And now he had to vacate it, having lost a legal battle to his nephew Manish, the son of his eldest brother Ram Prakash Gupta. He stared in the distance, his eyes glazed with a shocked sadness as he thought about the happy times when he and his brothers would sit in the flower-bedecked garden near the fountain, sharing a joke while sipping one cup after another of steaming, flavoured tea. Along with the daily news, they would discuss a variety of topics, smoothly transiting from politics to films to television serials to their work, and then back again to politics, but not necessarily in that order. It was a ritual they carried out every morning before going to their respective apartments to get ready for work. No day was complete unless it begun that way.

The four brothers—Ram Prakash, Atam Prakash, Suraj Prakash and Anand Prakash were the sons of Rai Saheb Shiv Shanker Lal Gupta. Their warm laughter and the joie de vivre they shared mirrored their camaraderie and the solidarity evident in their relationship. They were the envy of the neighbourhood, and theirs was a model family that many idolized.

They, like many others in Delhi who had come from across the border, had left their home and all their possessions in Pakistan during the Partition in 1947. They had lived in the refugee colonies of Rajendra Nagar and Krishna Nagar for sometime, and then making use of the Alternative Allotment Scheme under the Evacuee Properties and Rehabilitation Act, they had obtained the land at Hauz Khas Enclave in lieu of their residential house and properties in Sialkot that had become a part of Pakistan.

In 1948, Ram Prakash was barely eighteen years old, but being the eldest son, the responsibility of helping their father fell on him. Naturally, he was asked to fill the application form for the alternative plot in his own name. And so it happened that when Rai Saheb was allotted the plot, the lease deed was executed by the government in the name of Ram Prakash. In

1960, according to their father's wish, the brothers had four separate housing units constructed on the plot. Rai Saheb wanted each of his sons to have his individual residence, yet he also wanted the whole family to enjoy the comfort of living close to each other on the same property. Life went well for the Gupta family. The brothers worked hard and flourished in their respective fields. Each had his own business but for Atam Prakash, who was an IAS officer. They earned good money. Their children grew up and, with the passage of time, this younger generation stepped into their own respective careers. As the years rolled by, they were married and had their families. All the while the four brothers stood as, what they lovingly termed, four Ashoka Pillars. They were a rock-solid foundation to the progression of the family. If there were occasional squabbles between their wives or the children, these were quashed right away for the brothers had a determined understanding that their peaceful coexistence was not to be upset.

As luck would have it, in 1994 the brother of Ram Prakash's wife passed away. The cremation was performed in Delhi after which Ram Prakash and his nephew, his deceased brother-in-law's son, went to Haridwar to submerge the ashes of the departed in the holy Ganges. By the time the rites were completed, it was nearing nightfall. Ram Prakash suggested they stay on in the city and make their return journey the next morning. But the nephew, having come from America, was in a hurry. Now that the formalities were over and he had wasted enough time, he wished to return to Delhi immediately so he could take the next flight back to America. They left Haridwar as late as 9.00 p.m., and once on the highway the nephew repeatedly urged the driver to maintain the car on high speed. It was probably due to this constant wrangling that the driver, irked by the pressure, tried to overtake a vehicle without noticing an approaching truck. It was a head-on collision. The three occupants of the car were killed on the spot. That night of 31 May 1994 was one the family would never forget.

A few months after the demise of Ram Prakash, differences arose between the three uncles and the nephew. Manish sent legal notices to his uncles to vacate the units occupied by them at the Hauz Khas Enclave property. He had inherited the entire property—the land and the four units constructed there on the basis of their being in the single name of his father. Manish had his own plans. He was being offered a handsome sum of money by a real estate builder to agree to a collaboration and use the land for a lucrative project. To him, his uncles stood as stumbling blocks to a prosperous future. The uncles had, no doubt, built their individual units from their own resources, but in the records of the government authorities, Manish's father's name alone stood registered as the sole owner of the asset. Legally and technically, the law was with Manish, and even though morally and ethically he could not have been more wrong, his uncles could do nothing about it.

Manish was the first grandchild of his generation in the family; he was the 'darling' of his uncles. They adored him and had pampered every wish of his when he was a little boy. But they had never seen this side of him. Whether it had remained dormant or whether he was under the influence of his father-in-law who became his adviser after the demise of Ram Prakash, no one could tell. But being an advocate of repute, his father-in-law seemed to spearhead the case on behalf of him. It was on his behest that Manish filed the suit for eviction against his uncles, calling them illegal trespassers. A court battle ensued. In nine years the matter went to the Delhi High Court where—on the grounds of the ownership of the plot being in the name of Ram Prakash, Atam, Suraj and Anand were to vacate the premises. The three uncles of Manish approached the Supreme Court next, but in spite of engaging the best solicitors, not to mention the time and energy they spent, they lost in the apex court as well. The verdict of the Supreme Court was pronounced in 2004.

Looking back, Anand realized that the names of all the four sons of Rai Saheb should have been registered in the municipal records. But they had never thought of doing such a thing! They had never thought it necessary to put their trust on paper and were paying for it. Sadly, they had only themselves to blame. Now, as Anand reflected upon the life of the family, his youngest daughter Shalini, the fourth of his children, interrupted his reverie. She brought news of the arrival of the team from the movers and packers company that was to help shift their household items to the new residence they were renting in Green Park, not far from where they were currently. A second-floor unit, it was one-fifth the size of what had been their abode for four decades. They had already discarded many of their furniture pieces, assuming their new home would not accommodate all of it. Life was going to be very different, Anand thought and sighed. Atam and Suraj had moved to their respective homes in Greater Kailash a month ago; he was the last one to vacate. His heart was heavy for he had his plate already filled with challenges.

Anand dealt in the wholesale trade of motor spare parts and had a 400 sq. ft shop in the commercial area of Kashmere Gate in Old Delhi. His business had flourished for many years and he was considered a good businessman. However, due to a new government policy prohibiting trucks from plying on road for more than ten years, the demand for spare parts had reduced drastically. The new rule affected Anand's business and it no longer remained as lucrative as it used to be. On the personal front, too, Anand faced a crisis. He was being harassed for dowry by his son-in-law, Ramesh, who made regular and constant demands for both cash and kind through his wife Seema, Anand's eldest daughter.

As long as his business had been doing well, Anand had indulged his children, but in his present condition he expected them to understand his limitations. He was especially upset with Seema; he did not expect his own daughter to behave in this manner. His youngest daughter was still to be married. He and his wife, Raj Rani, were particularly worried about how they were to make arrangements for that occasion and had been trying to put aside whatever savings they could spare from time to time. Seema had been told by her parents, in no uncertain terms, that they were in no position to humour her anymore, but her demands were insatiable. Anand, Raj Rani and Shalini settled down in their new address and tried to make it their home. They curtailed much that they had been used to and opted for a simpler lifestyle. But life only got tougher for Anand. His business went from bad to worse. There were days when there was no sale at all. He was compelled to take stock of his costs for the first time in all the years of running his business, he had to lay-off a section of his employees whose salaries he could not afford any longer.

In the midst of this gloom, a relative of theirs, Ram Rattan arrived one evening at their home with a marriage proposal for Shalini. Lalit Aggarwal, the prospective match, had a degree in business management and worked with his father in their sanitary wares shop in Old Delhi. They lived in Pusa Road, and theirs was a well-to-do family worth considering.

During the next few days, Anand and Raj Rani pondered over and discussed the proposal. Though it seemed a sound and attractive offer, they were extremely apprehensive. What would the dowry demand be? In the Gupta circles, dowry was known to be a predominant feature of a wedding and, in fact, *the* consideration. The demand from a boy's family was, customarily, in accordance with the qualifications or the value attached to the boy. Anand feared that the call from Lalit's family would be high.

And so the discussions continued with Raj Rani continuously harping on Shalini's age. She was already twenty-nine and would soon touch thirty wailed the mother. If they delayed any further, it would be impossible to find a good groom for her. Raj Rani was also keen on the proposal for it meant that Shalini would continue to stay in Delhi after marriage. It was a plus point! She missed her second and third daughters—Sandhya lived in Hyderabad while Meera in Mumbai. It was not an easy decision for Anand. He was caught between his love for his youngest child, who had always been his favourite, and his own financial difficulties. Nevertheless, he finally decided to accept the proposal. He called Shalini to discuss the matter with her and she, who had been mentally prepared for marriage for some time now, was only too willing. She agreed immediately.

A meeting of the Guptas and the Aggarwals—Satya Pal and Santosh along with their son Lalit—was arranged in Ram Rattan's house. With one look at Shalini, Lalit took an immediate fancy to her. His consent was writ large and clearly on his smiling face, much to the annoyance of his mother. She darted looks of displeasure in his direction. He must not show such eagerness so soon, she silently opined. The evening went well for the two families who took to each other. They gave their approval by agreeing to meet yet again to take the talks further.

Anand now invited the Aggarwals to his residence to formally settle the alliance between the two families. During this second meeting, while Lalit and Shalini tried to get to know each other better, the parents and other elders sat in another room to discuss the intricacies of the dowry to be agreed upon between them. Santosh Aggarwal demanded fifty-one lakh rupees for her son and also that the amount be handed over to Lalit during the engagement-cum-tilak ceremony that was to be held first in four months' time. The other items—jewellery, clothing, furniture and electronics, as well as a new Honda City car—the boy's mother informed, could be handed over at the time of the wedding. She also made a list of her relatives who were to be presented with expensive tokens, and conveyed very sweetly that all the arrangements made should be of the highest standard possible.

After the Aggarwals had left and Anand sat back deep in thought, his wife joined him and together they deliberated upon the preparations that would be required for the occasion.

They weighed their resources. The bank deposit they had made in Shalini's name was badly depleted, a chunk of the savings having been used as payment towards the exorbitant fees of lawyers during the case. The main concern at the time of the engagement was the cash to be given; the marriage would not take place unless this symbolic sum was honoured. They needed to arrange for this amount first and then they would have six months to prepare for the expenses of the wedding.

Anand began making arrangements for his funds. He persuaded his friend Krishan Gopal—owner of K.G. Motors, the shop next door to his at Kashmere Gate—to purchase a half portion of his shop for thirty-five lakhs. In the depressed market conditions, it was the best price he could get. Anand also sold his shares and obtained a bank loan by hypothecating the stocks at his shop. But he was aware that he might still require more funds. So he spoke to his brothers who promised to help him if a deficit arose. Anand was relieved, at least for the present, for he had been able to raise the money crucial to the alliance. And since the bank loan, as well as the amount from the sale of shares and shop portion were received through the banking channel, Anand chose to have a demand draft made in the name of Lalit Aggarwal instead of arranging for cash. He placed the draft carefully in a fancy envelope, ready to be handed over during the tilak ceremony that would seal the alliance between the two families.

A day before the function, there was an excise department raid on the banquet hall reserved by Anand. As a consequence, it was sealed by government officers for violation of law by its owners. Anand was left in the lurch. At such a short notice, he had no choice but to either postpone the event or to move the venue to another location. In consultation with the Aggarwals, it was decided to organize the function at Anand's residence itself. The two families hurriedly shortened their guest lists, and Anand made arrangements for a count of sixty heads since only a limited number of people could be comfortably accommodated at the small flat. Atam and Suraj Prakash helped arrange for the buffet meal and the decorations.

The next morning, the Aggarwals and their relatives and friends arrived with a number far exceeding what had been decided upon. The apartment congested in no time, and some of the guests had to spread out to the balconies for want of space. Many of them found themselves standing. The living room was where the tilak ritual was to be held, but not all of the gathering could fit in there to witness the occasion. In all the anxiety of the sudden turn of events preceding the occasion, Anand had completely forgotten to mention a very significant matter to the Aggarwals or even Ram Rattan. It was significant not so much because he recognized it to be so but because of the effect the overlook created later, that instead of cash he had had a demand draft made. In hindsight, it was a blunder committed by him. Now, during the tilak, as the ritual was being observed, Anand placed the envelope in a basket of sweets that he presented to Lalit.

That was yet another lapse. He could have given the sacred envelope directly to Satya Pal or Santosh or Lalit, or at least have brought it to their notice that it rested in the basket of sweets...but he did not. Thereafter, one thing led to another. Lalit, completely unaware of the value of the basket that had been placed in his hands, handed it to a relative who handed it to another relative who placed it on a side counter in the midst of the other gift baskets of sweets and fruits that were being passed on. In the overcrowded room, with the guests rubbing shoulders with one another as well as the movement of the basket itself, the envelope dropped out and fell to the ground. No one noticed it. It could not have been more than a few minutes after the ceremony when there was complete pandemonium. Santosh Aggarwal, who had proudly articulated that her son was going to get a certain cash amount, waited expectantly for its appearance. Her guests strained their necks to look at the gifts being presented and gestured to each other— had it been given yet?

As boxes and hampers were handed over, Santosh grew increasingly impatient. The nods and expressions of her guests began to unnerve her. She had been dying to hold a thick wad of fresh bank notes in her hands; but when it seemed it was not to be, she was extremely annoyed. She assumed that the Guptas had gone back on their word. Without so much as asking Anand Prakash or Raj Rani for an explanation or even confronting them, she resorted to action that was uncalled for. She let a glass drop from her hand as though it were a mistake and urged her guests to put down their food. No one would partake of the meal spread out in their honour she instructed. Her relatives and friends obligingly followed her directive. Plates and glasses were pushed back on the tables, and food and drink splattered on the white linen as well as on the floor. Suddenly, the noise of sharp clanging and clinking of crockery and cutlery filled the air. The misbehaviour, totally unbecoming, took on an uglier turn when Santosh raised her voice and ordered Lalit to return the ring to Shalini at once. They were calling off the alliance, she shouted. Lalit was shocked. He could not react to this sudden outburst. Both he and Shalini looked at each other baffled, not knowing what to make of what was happening.

The guests, some amused at the goings-on, others sharing the frenzy of Santosh and Satya Pal, began to add to the noisy confusion. They had never heard or seen such a thing. They yelled and began criticizing the food, the lack of proper seating arrangement and the faulty air conditioning that was ineffective in the congested space. Some of them, egged on by the Aggarwals, began to leave the house. The laughter of a short while ago turned to verbal lashes bordering on abuse. Anand and Raj Rani were horrified. For a few moments confusion prevailed because they were unable to understand the real reason for the appalling and demeaning conduct of their guests. They tried to pacify the boy's side. Anand asked Satya Pal what had gone wrong even as Santosh furiously accused Raj Rani of not keeping her word. It was only when Satya Pal categorically mentioned the 'dowry' amount and accused Anand of not fulfilling his promise that the latter actually understood the situation. He acknowledged his mistake of not having informed them about the draft, but clarified that he had given it to Lalit in a gift envelope along with a basket of sweets. He then requested Santosh Aggarwal, with folded hands, to calm down and allow the function to continue. Santosh looked at Lalit, but he had no clue about the basket or the coveted envelope containing fifty-one lakhs.

Everybody moved towards the counter on which the sweets

and fruit baskets had been placed but no matter how hard they tried, they could not locate the envelope in any of the baskets.

Anand was certain he had given the envelope to Lalit, yet he went into his bedroom and checked his personal closets and cabinets, his table drawers and his briefcase. Even though he was sure not to find it in these places, he still hoped for it to appear from somewhere. He was puzzled; how it could have suddenly vanished, just like that! He and his wife checked all the possible places around the flat, but with no luck.

Satya Pal, though a timid man, lost his patience and asked Anand and Raj Rani to end their melodrama. He called out to Lalit to leave Shalini's hand and return the ring. All through the confusion, the just-engaged couple had been standing clutching one another, wondering what the end result of this chaos would be. Satya Pal turned to his guests, and apologizing profusely he asked them to proceed to the parking area. He was terminating the alliance, he said. His wife was even more dramatic in her behaviour. She pulled Lalit away from Shalini and with a flash of her fingers, wiped the tilak that had been applied on his forehead during the puja. He tried to protest, but his parents were in no mood for any reasoning. As they walked towards the door Anand and his brothers stood in the way, willing the Aggarwals to hear them out and believe in what they were saying. Anand pleaded that he was not lying and had sufficient proof to substantiate his claim that a draft had been made. How could he lie about a bank draft that could be proven! He pleaded with Satya Pal to stay. Finally, the boy's father agreed, saying he would hold his family for another fifteen minutes; but in case the demand draft was not found, there would be no further talk. They would leave for good and the engagement would stand cancelled.

The Guptas made a desperate attempt to look for the missing draft but it was to no avail. Nobody thought to look under the side counter. The Aggarwals and their guests stood on the road outside and waited, and when they heard of the failed search attempt, they carried on from there, fuming. The engagement, they were adamant, was called off!

Upstairs in the apartment, Raj Rani broke down. She cried bitterly. What had just taken place was unbelievable. Apart from the months of planning and the effort they had put in to arrange for the money, she could not believe that what had just occurred had to do with her own family, her own daughter. She felt ashamed and at a loss. Their guests stood around sympathizing, trying to help with the cleaning and restoring order in the living room which was a total mess. Of all the guests, one remained conspicuous by his behaviour—Ramesh. He sat in a corner, quietly watching the others. After some time, he left the house, leaving Seema behind with her parents. When the guests had left and they were all alone, Shalini put her head on her mother's lap and wept. She had come to like Lalit in the short time they had known each other. Poor Anand! It depressed him further. The insults, the embarrassment, and to see his loved ones go through such pain became unbearable. And then the inevitable happened. Suddenly he felt extremely unwell. The pain that seized his heart came all too sudden and he fell to the floor, unconscious. He was rushed to the hospital where he was admitted into the intensive care unit. Medical tests were carried out. They watched him closely for the next forty-eight hours, and though his condition stabilized, the cardiologist suggested that he undergo a surgical procedure.

In the coming days, Raj Rani, Shalini, as well as Sandhya and Meera, who had come to Delhi for the engagement, forgot about everything and concentrated on taking care of Anand's health. Seema and Ramesh, too, visited the hospital often and supported the ailing Anand. Something had changed for Ramesh and Seema ever since the day of Shalini's engagement. They were filled with disgust and remorse as they realized their own mistake. Ramesh now seemed a different person. He stood at the hospital reception throughout the first night, continuously asking the doctors and nurses after his father-in-law's health. The news of Anand's condition had alarmed him and made him feel very guilty about his own behaviour. He believed he had been no better than the Aggarwals and repented it. As Anand recuperated, Ram Rattan, taking Seema and Ramesh into confidence, suggested they pay a visit to the Aggarwals without letting Anand know. Several days had passed and it was possible that the Aggarwals had had a change of heart. He believed it was important that they reignite the alliance before the flames died down altogether.

The three of them went over to the Aggarwal home. It was a surprise visit, so they were glad to be allowed in. Ram Rattan informed the Aggarwals of Anand's condition and how his health had suffered because of what had transpired. He requested Satya Pal and Santosh to reconsider the relationship in spite of everything, especially since Lalit and Shalini had grown fond of each other. And though the draft could not be found, the bank had confirmed it had been issued in favour of

Lalit. They showed them a certificate to the effect.

But Ram Rattan had been mistaken; there was no change of heart. Santosh was not willing to relent. On the contrary, she stated that her son would not marry Shalini even if the draft were to be found. She had been insulted in front of her relatives who now gossiped that she had had no reason to boast because the Guptas had never intended to give any dowry. She was terribly upset and the situation, instead of a reconciliation, took a different turn. The Aggarwals accused Ram Rattan of conspiring against them and deliberately maligning their reputation. Ram Rattan was furious at the allegations and retaliated. The argument that followed ended with the representatives of the Gupta family being shown the door.

When Anand was discharged from the hospital, he remained in bed for some time. But the mystery of the missing draft haunted him terribly. So once his health showed considerable improvement, he had the house turned upside down and thoroughly searched under his own supervision. The furniture was moved and every nook and corner was carefully combed. This time they found the draft—it lay under the side counter in the living room, lodged between the unit and the wall. It must have lain there all along, probably kicked there by someone's foot once it had fallen to the floor. Anand was extremely relieved because it was proof of his honesty. Anand, taking his brothers along, went to visit the Aggarwals. He must absolve himself of their accusation, he thought, and give the relationship one more chance. Satya Pal met him properly and asked after his health, but he and his wife were surprised at the visit after what had transpired between them and Ram Rattan. When

Anand showed them the draft, Santosh reacted first. She did a complete volte-face, a complete turnaround. Suddenly, all was well. She accepted the inadvertent error and agreed to forget the past. With his eyes filled with tears and his hands folded, Anand thanked them wholeheartedly.

The two parties mutually decided to confirm a fresh wedding date after consulting the pundit. Anand also agreed to some conditions—to have Ram Rattan tender an apology for his misbehaviour (it was only then that Anand learnt about the incident, but since everything was freshly settled, he did not comment on it), to arrange for the wedding ceremony at a five-star hotel, and to bear all the expenses of the couple's honeymoon in Singapore. Back home, Anand gathered the family around and happily gave them the news. Raj Rani was very pleased, Seema and Ramesh were quiet, but it was Shalini's reaction that they had not anticipated. She was outraged, and for the next few minutes gave vent to her feelings. Everyone remained quiet as she rejected the agreement outright. 'How dare they!' she exclaimed. 'How dare they behave like this with us? Who do they think they are, especially that spineless Lalit? My father will not face any more humiliation, nor anyone else from my family for that matter. They should have apologized after seeing the draft instead of asking for more. And what if they make more demands even after the wedding?'

Shalini continued, tears streaming down her face as she stood in front of her elders. 'I refuse to marry into such a family. I will only marry someone I find worthy of my respect. Else, I will remain single!' As Seema and Ramesh rose and put their arms around her, Shalini turned to her brother-in-law and said, 'Ramesh bhaiya, please tell those wretched Aggarwals that I have said a big "no" to the marriage proposal. My father will not bow down to such people and bear further disgrace.' And then turning to her father she said, 'From now on, I will be your son. I will help you in the shop and give you the support you need. Please stop worrying about my marriage and let us work together to restore the business.'

The elders looked at each other. What was Shalini saying? Gupta girls did not speak like boys! Anand was the first to come around. Though he wanted with all his heart that Shalini settle down in life, he had borne enough embarrassment by the Aggarwals and was badly shaken as a result. Suddenly, he was ashamed of himself. He had got carried away in trying to 'settle' his daughter. Shalini's outburst now brought him back to his senses. He had not given her an education for nothing. She had a master's degree in commerce and was a confident individual. She could look after herself. He had no cause for worry. Anand hugged his daughter, very proud of the person she had become. The others nodded in agreement. Bewilderment turned to smiles. Yes, this was what the modern world was all about. And they would not give in to such demands!

Ramesh happily conveyed the message to the Aggarwals— they could look for another customer for their obedient son and sell him to another bidder in the market, he told them. The draft was cancelled and Shalini requested her uncle, who owned K.G. Motors, to let her buy back the space they had sold to him. She began going to the shop regularly. Steadily, Anand saw the trend change for them. The business began to stabilize and, with his beloved daughter by his side, Anand developed a renewed impetus towards his work. Shalini then bagged a sole-selling agency of Bosch Ltd for auto parts, and there was no turning back. Business went up the curve, and in two years' time the turnover crossed from double to many times.

Shalini's hard work and dedication were a surprise for many at Kashmere Gate. She had entered a field reserved solely for men; but when she proved her mettle and did exceedingly well, and that too when the line of business was seeing difficult times, there was admiration all around. Anand held his head high. She was his daughter, he declared proudly. He had completely recovered but was glad to have her as his able partner. He admitted to his wife—he could not have achieved what Shalini had managed to do.

Meanwhile, the past two years had been difficult for Manish. His father-in-law, his mentor, had died, and he had been badly duped. He had entered into an agreement with a real estate builder to begin a new project on the Hauz Khas Enclave address, but the latter had refused to pay him the agreed amount and had begun stalling the project. Manish had tried to rescind the collaboration agreement, but the builder would not agree to that either. He kept delaying the project, giving Manish one excuse after another, probably waiting for the market to pick up so he could make a better profit. For Manish, the experience was an eye-opener. He was forced to accept his mistake and he cursed himself for having held money more important than his family. The only people who could get him out of his present predicament were the ones he had unceremoniously thrown out of their own home. He genuinely lamented his ignorance and went forward to make peace with his uncles. Atam, Suraj and Anand were glad to see their family back as one. They took charge and set themselves up to deal with the builder. It took about eight months for matters to settle down before the brothers could once again start living in their former home. Even so, that did not deter them from visiting their home during the weekends, in the early morning, just to share their cup of tea together in the garden. Their laughter once again reverberated across their street, and it was louder than before, drowning once and for all the gossiping that had begun to do the rounds in the neighbourhood regarding their inheritance issue.

Shalini was a contented lady. After two years of sheer hard work she could now breathe easy. Business was working as she had planned, in fact better. She had not anticipated this level of success, nor could she now foretell how her life was about to change in the future. She had pushed the events of the past into the recesses of her mind, not wanting to ever think about what had happened. But one fine morning she received a telephone call from Lalit. He told her that in the two years gone by, he had kept himself informed of her whereabouts and activities, and he truly admired her grit and strength of mind. He had never given up on her as he had missed her all along. And after the ugly episode between their families, he had refused to consider any other proposal. He had worked hard to strengthen his individual standing, both emotionally and economically. He was now calling because he felt the time was right. Could she forget the past and marry him? Shalini could have been struck by a thunderbolt! Lalit proposing to her on his own merit was unbelievable. What about his parents? she wondered. Did they know? But Lalit was not the same person anymore. And he was very particular—there was to be no dowry! He was also clear that irrespective of what his parents said, he would not allow any interference from anyone this time round. His would be the final word. He went further to say that, he would try and stop the system of dowry, beginning with his own family. By the time he had finished, Shalini was reeling. She asked for some time to think. Her family must be consulted, she said. Then she put the phone down with a promise to call him back and a smile slowly spread over her flushed face.

The Wambesi Throne

In the southern part of the African continent, countries such as South Africa, Botswana and Angola had rich diamond mines. Congo, a country bordering these countries, did not boast of any such wealth. It was poor and it was controlled by the Belgians.

In 1915, Belgian and British geologists were exploring several parts of Congo looking for copper in the Shinkolobwe mines, when they chanced upon some earth on a hilltop that was stained with several colours. One such colour was a yellow which they knew to be associated with uranium. Curious as they were, they sent some rocks for tests to Belgium. To their amazement, the samples contained uranium at a level of 80 per cent—the purest concentration in the world. Uranium was an element much in demand in those days but it was not easily available. Hence, there was a huge price attached to it. And radium, being a by-product of uranium, was equally in demand for its use in medicine, especially cancer treatment. By chance, the Belgians and the British had struck gold in Congo. In a short time, they came back with a large contingent of their men for further exploration and excavation of this pure form of uranium.

On a particular evening as the sun descended in the sky, and even as a group of geologists spread across a hillside of Shinkolobwe, the sound of drums could be heard at the foot of the hills. Lights shone and festivities filled the air. The sound of voices singing grew louder and drumbeats spurred a gathering of tribesmen to a quicker dance around a huge fire.

King Wambesi sat on his throne, delighting in the celebrations organized to mark the birth of his son—his heir apparent and the future ruler of the Mwanga Tribe of Congo. The whole village was in a festive mood as men, women and children joined their king and the royal clan on the occasion of the arrival of Prince Wambesi. King Wambesi, one of the descendants of King Kongo-Dia-Nlaza, was the ruler and owner of the Shinkolobwe lands and forests. On that November evening of 1915, as he regaled himself, he was totally unaware of the rich find of uranium by the geologists on his lands.

Kongo-Dia-Nlaza was an ancient kingdom. It became part of the Kingdom of Kongo after the sixteenth century and came to be known as Kongo. When the Belgians took over and colonized the country, it was called Belgian Congo and, eventually, when it got its freedom from Belgium the name finally changed to a simple Congo. A majority of the population lived in remote areas in dense forests. From a nomadic life, they took to cattle breeding and farming. The descendants of King Kongo-Dia-Nlaza owned massive lands and agricultural produce was the main source of their income. Gradually, over centuries, their lands became fragmented and several small tribes became rulers of their own areas. Mwanga was one such tribe.

King Wambesi was a brave hunter. He was a strong man, yet

humble. In settling all matters concerning his tribe, he listened carefully to the advice of the wise old men amongst them. The tribe led a simple life. In those times, they did not have the comforts of electricity and motor vehicles, yet they were a happy and a contented lot. But things changed with the arrival of the unscrupulous foreigners who robbed their lands of its hidden wealth.

Once World War I was over, the Belgian and British geologists secretly informed the Americans of the presence of uranium in Congo. Recognizing the high-grade quality of the element, the Americans sent a contingent of people under the pretext of excavating copper. They hired men from the local tribe of King Wambesi and began the excavation of the mineral from the Shinkolobwe mines. During the mining process, safety of the environment was not ensured and this resulted in worker radiation exposure. The harmful effects of contaminated drinking water and polluted air led to severe health disorders and diseases that manifested fifteen years later.

Prince Wambesi grew up in his tribe listening to the glorious stories of his great ancestors who once ruled the kingdom. At the age of twelve, he was sent to Zaire for his studies. Here, for the first time in his life, he realized that there was more to the world than he had imagined. He was intelligent and curious, and being a quick learner with good grasping abilities, he soon proved to be an excellent student. As he grew into adulthood and became more aware of the happenings around the world, he was eager to learn and to acquire further knowledge.

His father sent him to America for his higher studies, and in 1937 he graduated in economics from the University of Iowa.

'Prince', as he was called by his schoolmates, was a kind soul. It was this quality that endeared him to everybody and made him popular in the university. Apart from enjoying the privilege of having a continuous flow of money sent by his father and which he shared with his friends, he made it a point to help those around him whenever he could.

It was Prince's last day at the university. Plans were afoot for the graduation party that evening when he was informed that he would have to rush home immediately. Prince bid farewell to his friends and took the first flight to Africa. He was required to change the aircraft and there were delays due to unavailability. Finally, when he arrived at N'djili Airport in Congo, he was shocked to see a group of his tribesmen waiting for him. He understood there was something gravely amiss. They broke the news to him gently. King Wambesi, his father, had contracted a fatal disease, and after suffering for the last six months had died three days ago. The same disease had also taken the lives of many of the tribesmen…almost two hundred. What was curious was that they were mostly men who had worked in the mines.

Prince's world changed in that instant. Overcome with grief and quite unable to comprehend the situation, he allowed himself to be led out of the airport and to his village. These were trustworthy people of his tribe, his own men who had watched him grow, and suddenly he felt himself leaning towards them for comfort. He was taken to the cemetery where the late king had been freshly laid to rest. Prince cursed himself. If only he had arrived earlier! He wanted desperately to see his father one more time, to speak with him one last time. As he knelt beside his father's grave, the tears began to fall and his whole body shook with anguish and disbelief.

There were rows of red iron crosses marking the graves—they were like miniature echoes of the iron superstructure of the uranium mines. On each grave stood a small white enamel food bowl, placed there to feed the ghosts so they would not leave the graveyard and return home. And each bowl had a hole drilled at the bottom of it to ensure no one stole it for reuse. It was an ancient ritual followed by the Mwanga Tribe. 'The King is dead! Peace be with the King!' As the air was rent with the calls of the subjects of the departed soul, Prince was devastated. The finality of his loss set in.

In the coming days, Prince tried to come to terms with his sorrow. It was a terrible setback, and suddenly his world at the university seemed far away. He had truly loved his father and held him in high esteem. Oh, the unfairness of it all! At twenty-two years, there was much that he had still wanted to learn from his father. Prince had looked forward to returning to his village, bringing with him the rewards of the modern world he had been exposed to. But what a return! The saddest moment in life, thought he, is when the person who gave you your best memories, becomes one himself! He now braced himself for what lay ahead. He knew that much against his will, he would have to take oath as king and assume his place on the Wambesi Throne. The coronation was conducted according to tradition. Thereafter, life changed course for the young King of Wambesi. There was nothing to do but accept his fate. Destiny had been cruel but he had to concede defeat in the hands of something much larger than his own plans. The young king knew that the tribe now needed their leader more than ever before. The disease that had inflicted the dead had brought poverty and suffering to many households. The situation needed to be remedied immediately or many families would perish completely. Perhaps fate had brought him back to his village to be the torchbearer of his people.

The young king now turned his heart towards the wellbeing of his tribe and accepted the responsibility of working for their improvement. Normalcy was required to be brought back as the first need of the hour, he acknowledged. His people must be made to feel safe and a means of livelihood be restored to the families affected so they could lead normal lives. Over the next few months, he learnt from his council of ministers about the American company responsible for the misery and death of his people—De Villiers Mining Corporation. They had not complied with the radioactive material mining safety standards. They had engaged US marine soldiers to ensure the excavation of the highest possible volume of uranium to be exported to the US for its Manhattan Project. America was establishing uranium enrichment plants and needed the element at any cost; even if the cost involved exposing a living tribe to the devastating effects of their activities. And compared with the rich haul De Villiers had taken, they had paid peanuts as compensation for mining on the tribal lands. The innocent tribesmen had been taken advantage of, they had been forced to work round-the-clock in the Shinkolobwe mines and paid meagre wages. Further, their lives had been ruined by exposure to the pollution and disease that wreaked havoc in the village. The young king learnt of the dreaded disease: cancer. It had taken the lives of his beloved father and the tribesmen. And all of it had been done intentionally and with the full compliance of the US government.

What he could not come to terms with was that while all this was happening to his own people in his beloved country, he had been on the shores of America, enjoying the abundance the country had to offer. He wanted revenge. Further, the uranium that was taken from Shinkolobwe actually belonged to him and his tribe, for he owned the hills. The perpetrators would have to pay for this, the young king promised himself, and he began a countdown to the day when he would settle scores.

He would sit for long hours on his throne, thinking in silence about life in general, and it all seemed ironic. A certain realization came to him—that silence is never empty, it is full of answers, and that it takes sadness to know real happiness, noise to appreciate silence, and the absence of a person to value his presence. He would cry bitterly at the loss of his father and his men. Time went by but the emptiness grew. The people of the Mwanga Tribe tried getting their lives back to normal, but an underlying sadness remained, threatening to stay there forever.

During World War II, industrial production increased drastically. After Malaysia fell to the Japanese, Belgian Congo became a strategic supplier of rubber to the allied forces. The young King Wambesi, sensing an opportunity for economic benefit due to the heavy demand, supplied produce from his rubber trees to put his tribesmen back on their feet financially.

In August 1945 when America dropped atom bombs on the Japanese cities of Hiroshima and Nagasaki killing thousands of innocent civilians and affecting millions, news spread of the uranium used for the bombs having come from none other than the Shinkolobwe mines. The pictures of Japan showing people dying and being crippled by radioactive effects revived the young king's sad memories of 1937. It urged him to put the rest of his plans to action and get even with the culprits who had inflicted great devastation on his tribe.

King Wambesi gave one long look at his throne—it was a single wooden structure. Having been used from the time of his ancestors, it was two hundred years old. The arms were inscribed with the names of his forefathers and had two skull-like figures carved on the ends. It was a unique traditional piece, preserved very carefully by the king's men who held it in great reverence because it stood as a mark of their roots and identity. And irrespective of its price in the market, for the king and his tribe the worth of the throne lay in its antique and emotional value. For them it was priceless!

The young king booked his air ticket from Kinshasa Airport to New York City. He was dressed in his forefathers' traditional leopard-skin attire and carried his throne along with him on his journey. On his arrival at La Guardia Airport in New York, he behaved in a manner typical of a native king from Africa, taking special care of the proper transportation of his throne. The customs authorities were intrigued by the tribal king, his mannerisms and his clothes, and passed him off as an eccentric royal figure from the African continent. Once in the city, the king's staff arranged his meetings with several important people including the ex-mayor, Fiorello La Guardia, to discuss matters of trade and economic opportunities between the countries. Now that the war was over, it was the time for development, and countries looked to establish trade opportunities with one another. All his meetings were held in the house he had rented, and the king insisted on sitting on his throne through all the talks. He must meet like a 'king' he insisted.

After the success of his first trip in 1946, King Wambesi made plans for a second one. His only problem was transporting his throne from Kinshasa Airport. During those times, corruption was rampant and no baggage could be taken on board unless padlocked. These could be purchased from porters but at a high price and all checked-in baggage carried charges. The Congolese loadmasters habitually took bribes and thus overloaded planes to the extent that there were instances when an aircraft would not lift off a short runway due to overloading. One airplane skidded off the end of a runway into a cluster of shanties that was not supposed to be there in the first place, killing dozens of Rwandan Hutu refugees. Under those circumstances it was difficult to transport his throne without damaging it. Determined though, the king undertook his second trip to New York. Wanting more publicity this time, he hosted a large banquet in a luxury hotel opposite Central Park in Manhattan and invited the important people of the city. His efforts resulted in widespread coverage by the media, and his photograph—seated on his throne—appeared in major tabloids. The Americans loved it; they loved an eccentric king squandering money in their country. And King Wambesi loved being noticed.

On his next trip, King Wambesi was in the news for another reason. Kinshasa Airport officials had failed to check the hand baggage of a local smuggler who had hidden a baby crocodile in it. There was pandemonium when the crocodile escaped from the bag during the flight and an uproar occurred on the plane. The king's men, adept at handling the species, helped restore order in the craft by securing the creature back inside the bag. Some people were injured, but the plane landed safely at its destination.

Now the young king had learnt that in the past few years, the diamond mines owned by the De Beers Company in South Africa were heavily insured and any mishap would result in the insurance company, De Villiers, paying out millions of dollars to the insured. De Villiers Mining Corporation had earned huge sums in the illegal export of uranium from his hills, and they were now spread all over the world and into the businesses of banking and insurance as well. When World War II ended, contrary to everyone's expectations, the American economy was booming. Corporate giants had made money from manufacturing defence goods and had shifted business to other sectors. De Villiers was one such giant.

The next time he travelled, the young king took a decision. He approached De Villiers and other insurance companies to insure his throne against 'wilful damage' for a massive sum of one hundred million dollars! The insurance companies were amused, being now acquainted with the idiosyncrasies of the leopard-skin-dressed eccentric king, and they asked for astronomical premiums. De Villiers, too, quoted a hefty sum of one hundred and twenty-five thousand American dollars as annual premium, believing the king was out of his mind and would not accept it. But King Wambesi agreed to sign a contract with them. He bought the insurance and consented to pay the said premium amount.

For the next two years, the young king paid regular visits to New York City, each time transporting his throne along with him. And during that time, he continued to pay the insurance premium. All the visits were costing him a lot of money, but the young king had by now become a master schemer, a fox who was remarkably shrewd in his approach. Prior to his next visit, he asked his close confidants to arrange for cocaine, and mixing it in a tank filled with warm water, he submerged his throne in it. The journey to New York Airport was uneventful, but the hullabaloo began at the New York customs checkpoint in the cargo division. The sniffer dogs picked up the smell of cocaine in the packed box containing the throne. As the canines began barking madly, the customs officials held the king and his royal entourage for a thorough checking. They could not find any contraband item in the possession of the king or any of his staff or, for that matter, hidden in the throne container. However, they were not satisfied. They smelt something fishy. Suspecting that the young king was carrying drugs inside the throne, they summoned the anti-narcotic cell. King Wambesi explained at length that the throne was over two hundred years old and carved out of a single piece of wood; hence, it had no cavities. But the authorities would not relent. They decided that the only way to unearth the drugs was to break the throne into pieces. The king warned them—the throne was an ancient relic and could not, under any circumstance, be broken. When the authorities insisted, the king prevailed that under the laws of the land, he must be allowed to call his attorneys and insurance company, De Villiers, and have them witness the 'wilful damage' to his ancestral heirloom.

The anti-narcotic wing consulted the insurance company and was informed that if the throne were found carrying drugs, there would be no liability on the company.

A scene ensued thereon. Various other airport officials gathered in the customs office to witness the interesting, albeit strange happening, the likes of which had never been seen before. In the presence of the agents from the insurance company, the customs authorities began dismantling the royal throne part by part. Every bit was thoroughly checked for the presence of cocaine, but nothing could be found in spite of breaking the structure into the smallest of pieces. All that was left of the royal seat was dried wood. The authorities could do nothing but release the king. The damage was done! Through a high profile attorney, King Wambesi filed a claim of one hundred million dollars on De Villiers, and on being refused, filed a suit in the New York law courts. He promised his attorney 7 per cent of the claim as fees. A legal battle arose as the insurance company did not want to pay a colossal amount for what they believed had been a worthless wooden structure.

Ultimately, the court ruled in favour of King Wambesi. The fact of the matter was that the Wambesi Throne had been more than two hundred years old and was used as the seat of power by the many kings of the Mwanga Tribe. The intrinsic, antique and ancestral value attached to it could not be ignored and demanded consideration. Further, the insurance company had agreed in writing to pay if the throne were wilfully damaged. The court now instructed De Villiers to pay the insured amount, plus the interest and legal charges to the king.

In the evening of the day the case was closed, a lone figure strolled towards the Bayonne Bridge in New York. Holding his jacket collars to his chin against the cold breeze, he could have been any one of the city's young men out on a walk. But King Wambesi was there for a reason. It was something he had wanted to do since his first visit to the US. The Bayonne Bridge was the largest and longest steel arch bridge in the world completed in 1931, connecting Staten Island in New York to New Jersey. A three-storied warehouse stood in the shadow of the bridge. It had stored vegetable oils until the day a ship owned by De Villiers Mining Corporation, carrying twelve hundred tons of raw uranium from Belgian Congo, had unloaded there. The uranium was later sold for the Manhattan Project that was responsible for making the atomic bombs.

Standing on the bridge and looking in the direction of the warehouse, the young king had tears in his eyes. The uranium stocked in that very warehouse a decade or so ago was brought from his own lands. It had been stained with the blood of his beloved father and his many tribesmen, not to mention the thousands killed by the bombing of Hiroshima and Nagasaki.

He had taken his revenge. He had deliberately made those trips to New York as a build-up to the finale. De Villiers had finally paid, at least in part, thought the king, for their wrongful actions. He could not bring back his father and his tribesmen who had lost their lives, however, he had got justice in his own way. For a moment the young king thought whether he had done the right thing, then he shrugged the feeling off. He was being true to his tribe and that was what mattered.

After settling his dues in New York, King Wambesi transferred his millions of dollars to his bank in Katanga, Congo, and flew to Kinshasa with his tribesmen. Immediately, thereafter, he set about utilizing the money as funds to create a better life for his people. He was a great leader and he ruled wisely. Only, it was minus his regal throne.

An Accomplisher

Himachal Pradesh, a northern state in India, is home to many scenic towns sprinkled across the folds of its hills. Each one of these beautiful towns offer travellers wondrous sights to behold. Barot is one such gift of nature. Tucked away between parts of the Dhauladhar Range of the Himalayas, in a small v-shaped valley formed by the river Uhl, this fascinating town lies in the district of Mandi. Popular in current times as a holiday location, it was relatively unknown when I first visited the place in 1984. And it was during that first visit to Barot that I was introduced to Colonel Sir B.C. Batty.

It all began soon after my wedding. My wife and I were invited by my brother-in-law Sushil Khanna, who was chief engineer with Punjab State Electricity Board (PSEB), to visit his home in Barot. Sushil is the husband of my wife's elder sister, and since they are an extremely charming and pleasant couple, we accepted the invitation gladly. We set about readying ourselves for the trip, looking forward with eagerness for a chance to go up to the hills.

We travelled by train from Delhi to Chandigarh, and on the

onward journey to the town of Joginder Nagar, we went by the car that Chief Sahib, as Sushil was popularly known, had sent for us. In those years, Barot was not accessible by road. It was a journey to be made mainly on foot from Joginder Nagar—a twelve-kilometre stretch through terraced fields and thick cedar forests inhabited by wildlife. There had been horrific instances of attacks on poor labourers and villagers by predators, so it was mandatory for visitors to have an escort to go along with them. An armed guide from the forest office was sent to accompany us in case a situation arose that demanded our protection.

With a little anxiety, we started the third leg of our journey from Joginder Nagar to Barot. Our guide or saviour as the trek would establish, led the way. Our bags were carried by an attendant while I carried a rucksack; and as I assessed my surroundings, I cursed myself for not having paid attention to my telephonic conversation with my brother-in-law when he gave me the details of the travel. It had all seemed as easy as he explained it but now, as I trudged along, I questioned my own wisdom for not being mentally prepared for the perilous condition of the route. However, the pure scenic beauty of the snow-covered mountains coupled with the gushing of flowing streams, soon melted my heart away. It took us close to four hours to cover the distance of the hilly terrain. There were stretches that required us to ride on a haulage trolley from the British times and, though it was meant to facilitate our journey, it actually challenged the spirit of adventure in me to the extreme. The open trolley moved on a rail track that was quite steep in certain areas, and it was indeed a miracle we did not go flying down into the ravine and the river flowing a hundred metres below. At times the trolley had to be manually pushed by our baggage bearers, the climb being difficult for it to carry all our weight. In those stretches, we hiked it. All in all, it turned out to be a hair-raising yet thrilling experience for us, and luckily our journey met with no untoward incident and we arrived at Barot safe and sound.

Once in the town, we were taken to the PSEB guest house for the customary rest after our long journey. However, to my astonishment, I felt as fresh as ever. The British era guest house, built on a plateau, faced the famous Barot waterfall, and I was involuntarily drawn to the glorious views it offered. As I filled my lungs with gulps of fresh and cool mountain air, I swept my gaze around in wonder. The town sparkled a blue-green hue after a spell of fresh snow and the wonderful weather infused an invigorating pleasantness in the air. My eyes took in the beautiful snow peaks and the hills around, and I was thankful that a court order prohibited any act of excavation on the hills. The beauty of Barot would remain untouched.

I was immersed thus, completely lost in my thoughts, when our relatives Sushil and his wife Meenakshi walked in. There were greetings exchanged and they enquired if we were comfortable. Yes, we said, we were more than comfortable and we thanked them sincerely for their warm gesture. If it had not been for their invitation, we would probably have missed out on visiting such a lovely place. We looked forward to a splendid stay over the coming days.

Lunch was served in the dining hall—special North Indian cuisine prepared under the able instructions of my sister-in-law. It was delicious to say the least, and I was enjoying my hot meal when I noticed a huge portrait of a British soldier adorning the wall above the mantel shelf. On my enquiring, my host informed me that the picture was of a Colonel Sir B.C. Batty—the gentleman responsible for installing the hydropower plant at Barot.

Post lunch and a short siesta later, we were at the neighbouring marketplace—the only one in Barot. The town boasted of a restaurant called Sher-e-Punjab and a small tea shop that was situated on a cliff facing the plant. We strolled across to the tea shop, and as we were enjoying some ginger tea along with locally baked garlic and cinnamon-flavoured biscuits, my eyes fell, for the second time that day, on a torn photograph of Colonel Sir Batty inaugurating the hydro plant on 15 August 1932. Though worn out and now pale in colour, the picture-frame seemed to have been given pride of place as it was hung on the wall of the main counter. My curiosity aroused, I wondered why a person responsible for initiating a project should be remembered in that fashion by a tea stall owner. The latter informed me that if I were to visit the houses of Barot as well as those of the neighbouring villages of Punjab and Himachal Pradesh, I would find a photograph of Colonel Sir Batty gracing a wall in almost each one of them. The inhabitants of that entire region believed he had been god-sent. I was truly intrigued. What had the British 'Batty' done to win such reverence? And how was it that we, the residents of the capital, Delhi, had never ever heard of him?

On our way back to the guest house, I flooded my brother-in-law with questions. Sushil told us that Sir Batty was an electrical engineer during the British Raj in India who had dared to defy the might of the British Empire. Against all odds, he had ushered in a new era in the lives of the people dwelling in the towns and villages within the five-hundred kilometre area that encircled Barot; and he had lived up to his promise of bringing electricity to their homes. It was now fifty-two years since that time, but the poor villagers of the area celebrated him as a hero for illuminating their lives. It was an interesting story, Sushil said, but being a long one it would require a couple of hours to narrate. We decided to spend the next morning on Colonel Sir B.C. Batty and his endeavours five decades back.

As planned, after breakfast the next day, Sushil and his wife joined us for coffee at the guest house. He began with a caution of truth. The story, having been passed over the years by word of mouth, had no written evidence to support it. No validation existed, Sushil said. He himself had heard it from his domestic help whom he called Ramu Kaka.

Colonel Sir B.C. Batty, as the story went, was an electrical engineer with a degree from The School of Electrical and Electronic Engineering at the University of Manchester, United Kingdom. Having attained his qualification, he became involved in establishing power plants in Manchester—a city that boasted of very large handloom units that required a steady supply of electricity to produce its cotton and yarn. In 1910, during the British Raj in India, Colonel Batty was appointed to join the engineering division for a project to construct a power plant near the river Ravi in Lahore, Pakistan. Scheduled to begin construction, the plant was proposed to be made operational by 1920. The pace of work during those days was such that a power plant project took a minimum of ten years to get commissioned.

First, the houses and utility areas were constructed and then the turbines were installed and connected with the transformers and transmission machines. Civil engineers and sub-divisional officers led the operation and positioned hundreds of workers to execute the construction of the residential as well as the commercial and production areas. The work of the electrical engineers came afterwards—to make the plant functional and generate electricity. Colonel Batty was involved in the Lahore mega project from its preliminary stages when the drawings were being readied.

Colonel Batty had a friend, John Truman, a designated site inspector, who was in charge of identifying sites in India where power plants could be established for the generation of electricity and its supply to various cities and towns. During the British rule, an important endeavour had been to provide electricity to major cities like Delhi, Bombay, Lahore, Madras and Amritsar. Villages appeared last on the agenda. Now, John was scheduled to visit the hills of northeast Punjab (of which Himachal Pradesh was a part at that time) to look for a hydro-generating power plant site and he asked Colonel Batty to accompany him. Batty accepted the invitation and together they travelled to various sites. The two men were mesmerized by the breathtaking views of the Himalayan Range, not to mention the beauty of Beas River. They spent three months looking for a suitable location for the power plant and it was then that they selected the 56-metre waterfall at Barot, flowing from Uhl River. The sheer force of the falling water caught their attention—it would be an ideal spot, they thought, to set up the turbines for generating electricity.

They prepared a report and submitted it to their superiors, but the latter did not express any interest in the project and the report was relegated to banked files. A disappointed Colonel Batty returned to Lahore and to the work being carried out at the plant at Ravi River. For the next two years he remained there, involved in the project. In the year 1912, John once again approached the resident commissioner for the Barot project and showed him the site. This time the latter, who knew John well, gave his approval. He called for a meeting with the project head, Sir Walter Scott, and asked him to initiate the plan at Barot. When Colonel Batty was informed about it, he immediately moved an application for his posting to the site. It was accepted and he was transferred to Barot.

Barot in those days was a remote, tiny village. It was inaccessible by road. The terrain being what it was, the construction of a roadway to facilitate the project wasn't considered feasible. It was decided to install a twelve-kilometre haulage trolley system instead, to facilitate the transport of construction material from Joginder Nagar to Barot for making a large water reservoir at Barot. The haulage design was a unique one. It ran on a rail track and also on a pulley structure that moved when people on opposite hills signalled to each other by pulling at the ropes. The drawings were prepared and the plan was sanctioned by the Viceroy in Delhi. The entire project was going to cost a whopping amount of ten lakh rupees, spread over a period of eight years—from 1912 to 1920. Certain parties in the British Government, who wanted that electricity be made available in and around the big cities first, opposed the venture. However, the project broke ground and the first of the funds—

two lakh rupees, was sanctioned from the treasury.

The residents of the neighbouring villages—Tikkan, Ghatsani and Silbandhwari—looked forward to the setting up of the power generating plant with anticipation, for it was to illuminate their homes and lives as well. Given the extent of work that entailed, plentiful hands were required, both skilled and unskilled. Requisitions were made to each and every village in the area. Villagers were informed and their support was sought for the successful completion of the project. In addition, labourers from distant locations—Mandi, Palampur, Kangra, Pathankot, Kullu and others—also came to Barot and were appointed.

The work for the reservoir at Barot and the power house at Joginder Nagar moved at a swift pace. Five years passed. During that period, Colonel Batty received six lakh rupees in funds and it was spent judiciously. At that stage of the work, it was envisaged that the project would take another four years to complete. By then, Colonel Batty had garnered a lot of respect due to the zeal and efforts he exhibited towards the completion of the power plant. He was also respected because unlike most of his fellow British men, though he was a faithful Christian he respected the local religious sentiments. He was known to be a thorough gentleman, one who would not hurt even a fly. He displayed the utmost respect for his subordinates and celebrated Hindu festivals with them.

However, the times changed. It was in 1916 that the adverse impact of World War I cut through the dreams and plans of Colonel Batty. The British Empire started facing trouble from all quarters and, as a consequence, India was directly affected.

Financial requirements of the war compelled the Governor General of India to reconsider the completion of the projects at Lahore, Barot and the various infrastructural schemes being carried throughout India. Money constraints were imposed. Rather, it was the Queen who asked for financial support from the Governor General of India. The world and work of Colonel Batty came to a standstill. He was informed by his accountant that their funds would cover costs only for the next two months. They needed to replenish their coffers immediately. With no scope of doing so from any other quarter, Colonel Batty made a trip to Delhi to meet his seniors. He wished to convince them about the need to complete the project at Barot. Instead, he was instructed firmly by Sir Humphrey, a senior officer for projects in India, that he was to not only shelve the project till the wretched war was over, but he was also supposed to lay off all the workers immediately. He was given orders to disband all the units working on the project. Further, he was also asked to enrol, either voluntarily or by force, his labourers in the British army so that they could be sent to the war front. It was a shock to Colonel Batty. He returned from Delhi utterly disheartened. However, he did not compel any person to join the British army nor did he retrench them. He did not have the heart to do such a thing. Over time, he had grown fond of his workforce, and that was very important to him. He carried on the work and continued to compensate the labour force—out of the available funds at first and, subsequently, from his personal reserves. The news spread like wildfire to all the villages and towns around. People were overwhelmed by Colonel Batty's dedication towards them. They began to visit the project area for a glimpse of the extraordinary man who dared to defy his British seniors.

Villagers and farmers of Punjab put their heads together. They held meetings, formed committees and sent ten people from each village to help and support Colonel Batty. Help came in many forms—be it as sacks of wheat and rice to feed the workers, or as cooks themselves offering assistance, or even as utility workers. People voluntarily extended themselves to Colonel Batty to support his cause and to help him achieve his goal—all for no payment in return. They refused to accept a salary for the work they were doing. That gesture of the local people reinforced Batty's sense of commitment to his work, and he continued to toil for the project's completion.

The war, however, began to take its toll. As for Colonel Batty, his attitude along with the unity and loyalty shown by the Indians towards him enraged the British government. Sir Humphrey and Sir Walter Scott were extremely displeased when they were informed about the supporters that he had gathered. Colonel Batty was becoming increasingly revered—like a living legend. It did not bode well for the British.

They took action. They dismissed all the government employees on work on the power project and issued orders for the transfer of Colonel Batty and John Truman to Calcutta to build barracks and support the army establishment there. In response, Colonel Batty submitted his resignation. He resolved to complete the project at Barot all by himself, on his own merit. It was a risky decision. On the one hand it defied the might of the British empire and on the other, there was no funding to help him. Without the support of the government, he knew it would be challenging to take the project to completion, especially since installing turbines and transmission wires required government sanctions.

Colonel Batty's decision had other repercussions. Revolutionaries as well as a certain political party used the news of his defiance to embarrass the British government. Various newspapers covered the story of his audacity and it became the talk of the times. When Her Majesty's government in London got wind of it, a summon was immediately sent to the Indian government to use force and stop the work at all costs. Colonel Batty, his associates and the poor labourers were taken under arrest and put behind bars at the Lahore Central Jail.

The headlines of the local newspapers splashed the news, covering the story of the brave British soldier and his men, and how they were tortured and imprisoned in spite of their good deeds and intentions. This added further fuel to the rumours being circulated by the revolutionaries—that the British were inhuman and harsh in their treatment of even their own people, especially to those who wished to do good for the Indians. They propagated that the unscrupulous foreigners be removed from the Indian soil forever.

Colonel Batty was produced in the Lahore courts. The judge presiding over his case was astonished to see the large local crowd of five thousand people gathered there to hear the case against the Colonel. And unlike most occasions, the halls of the courts on that day echoed slogans in favour of a British person as against the usual cries in favour of Indian leaders. Colonel Batty's popularity had, in effect, assumed greater heights after his arrest. The more the British criticized him, the more the local populace admired him. In prison he had become a larger force to reckon with.

The judge could not find any provision, under any of the Acts in force, to stop a person from using his own funds to carry out social work or to try to complete a project for the good of the people of the country, yet he was inclined towards the government lawyer, a British person who pressed charges against Colonel Batty. The latter was accused of using government assets—the machines and equipment installed at Barot being the property of the government—to continue work on the plant against orders. He was also accused of using the service of government staff and continuing to stay at the government accommodation. The prosecution argued that the Colonel be barred from doing any further work on the hydro plant at Barot.

On his part, Colonel Batty argued in person and politely told the judge that his intention had never been to disrespect his superiors. He said he had made considerable progress on the project and believed that at that juncture, a sanction of two lakh and fifty thousand rupees was all he needed to complete the work. He was very close to his objective of generating electricity for the people who lived in the region. He wished to be allowed to carry on, but his request was declined.

The matter was transferred to the district court at Shimla. Colonel Batty tried to reason his case, saying the machines could not be removed without causing permanent damage to them. He argued that the British government was being biased, and that the action sought by them would result in losing much more than any gains accruing to them. The judge, who had no sympathy for the illiterate, ugly, brown-skinned natives of

Barot, gave an adverse judgement. He released the Colonel on bail but barred him from continuing work on the project. He also gave a ruling that the government be allowed to remove the installed equipment.

On hearing of Colonel Batty's release from prison, people were overjoyed. Little did they realize that he had been forbidden from accomplishing his dream project. They cheered for him, the air resounding with their deafening cries, much to the awkwardness of the British judge, the other British police officers as well as Sir Humphrey and Sir Walter Scott present in the court.

Not one to be deterred yet, Colonel Batty approached Shimla High Court through an experienced lawyer. The latter worked painstakingly on the case, researching the Privy Council case laws and arguing the case s, that the hostile British media began reporting the court proceedings verbatim. Praise for Colonel Batty's determined efforts at Barot began to appear in the papers and the press became increasingly absorbed as the case unfolded.

The court verdict, this time, went in favour of Colonel Batty. It was a landmark victory—one hailed as one of the best-fought legal battles of those times. A ruling against the British government was unheard of in the early twentieth century in India.

The Shimla High Court, however, decreed that though Colonel Batty was being permitted to complete the project through his own resources, the land, equipment and 50 per cent of the electricity generated would belong to the British government. Colonel Batty accepted the verdict. He made no further appeal. As for the British government, it was advised not to pursue the matter any further for fear of making Colonel Batty still more popular. The Colonel then faced the uphill task of procuring funds to meet the huge deficit—two lakh and fifty thousand rupees. He approached the Maharajas of Patiala and Kapurthala, the richest states of North India in the 1920s, but he was politely refused any help since the Indian Rajas did not wish to annoy the British. Colonel Batty, assisted by a few of his staunch supporters who had their hearts firm on achieving freedom for their country, then sent out an appeal to the people of India to donate for their cause. Donations began to pour in. These were more from ordinary people who were near poverty themselves and so they had nothing to fear. Most of the rich did not venture any support, for they did not wish to invite the British ire. The rich of Indian society were happy to be on the side of the British government—it meant being conferred with the titles of Rai Bahadur and Rai Sahib that the British awarded them when pleased.

Colonel Batty went from one village to another personally, collecting whatever help he could. After an exhausting tour of Punjab and Uttar Pradesh, he managed to put together some funds. However, he still remained short by one lakh and seventy-five thousand rupees. Due to the delay in work on the project and court battles, the original cost as perceived had escalated. Colonel Batty had not anticipated such an occurrence. He decided on a bold action. Leaving the work to the responsibility of John and other volunteers, he set sail on a twenty-one day journey to London and then travelled onward by train to Manchester where he owned a house and other lands bequeathed to him by his grandfather. The assets, if sold, were deemed to fetch him enough money to cover the deficit he faced.

Colonel Batty's arrival in England's Port of Dover was met with disapproval. He was scorned at and questioned unnecessarily by the authorities as if he were an Indian slave of theirs. Some hurled abuses at him, yelling at him to go back to India. At the Manchester railway station, however, he was warmly welcomed by a group of Indians who were aware of his efforts back home.

During the course of his stay Colonel Batty bore the insults that were directed his way, even as he approached people to buy his properties and other assets. After great anxiety and at a price much lower than the evaluated rate, he was able to make a sale and remit one lakh and fifty thousand rupees to his bank in Lahore. He returned to India after three months. The work had made slow progress under John but what was encouraging was the presence of a new force of young men working on the project free of charge. They were educated but it was the surge of patriotic temper that engulfed the youth in those times that had driven them to make their contribution to the development of the nation.

Colonel Batty was overwhelmed by such acts of support. In spite of various incidents of sabotage on the project that time and again were perpetrated by those wanting to hinder his progress, the love shown to him by his people kept him going. He received help in the form of both labour as well as small funds from time to time and that motivated him to keep his eyes on his goal.

However, circumstances being what they were, the project was delayed. The war and his legal battles threw Colonel Batty back by many years. The decade of the 1920s came and went. Finally, on 15 August 1932, the plant at Barot—the first hydro-electric project in northern India—was inaugurated. It was attended by two hundred thousand natives and nine British officers.

The illumination that was created had the rich and the poor people across northern India, especially undivided British Punjab, rejoicing. It was akin to their celebrating the festival of lights, Diwali. As a consequence of the project, most areas of north and northwest India received electricity. It changed their lives forever. Those who had been used to hand-operated fans and mashals (a kind of fire torch for illumination), could now think of working till the late hours after sunset while using machines and gadgets to help in their progress. Things that were till then unheard of became a reality in people's lives.

The newspapers carried front page stories of Colonel Batty's feat. It was nothing less than superhuman, they said, and he was respected and revered accordingly. People began to almost worship him. For them he was god-sent. Every home began to have a portrait of his, and they acknowledged that he had spent twenty-years of his life for them.

The British remained cold towards Colonel Batty. They ignored his mammoth achievement and proclaimed it a work done by a mad and arrogant man who thought no end of himself. Sir Humphrey had by then become advisor to the Governor General of India in Delhi. In fact, both he and Sir Walter Scott had become very powerful with the passage of time. And just as the government had a score to settle with the anti-British Batty for undermining the mighty British authority, Sir Humphrey and

Sir Walter Scott too had not forgotten the insult meted out to them by the electrical engineer, their subordinate. His project at Barot had far outshone their power plant project at Lahore, and they were jealous of his popularity.

It was not as though Colonel Batty had ever expressed a contempt for his authorities, even though he disliked the manner in which native Indians were treated by his fellowmen. Personally, he made no distinction in his treatment of Indians and despised reservations against them. He would have nothing to do with it. He enjoyed their company and even visited their homes, often dining with them. That behaviour of his did not carry favour with the British, who believed in maintaining a certain distance from the natives.

Sir Humphrey and Sir Walter Scott hatched a conspiracy that was endorsed by their higher authorities. They called Colonel Batty to Delhi to meet the Governor General of India and presented him the honourable title of 'Sir'. Colonel Batty became Colonel Sir B.C. Batty. As he strode the immaculate lawns of the residence of the Governor General at Raisina Hill and viewed the newly-built India Gate—a war memorial for the Indian soldiers who had laid down their lives during the world war—Colonel Sir Batty was at last a happy man. He believed that his efforts were being acknowledged by his seniors. He did not suspect anything. That was not all. He was also provided with a new Rolls-Royce car along with a chauffeur, a young and jovial British fellow called Michael who was ordered to take his instructions of duty from Colonel Sir Batty and to serve and report to him.

Colonel Sir Batty returned home in his new car with

Michael. It took them three full days for the drive back. They parked the vehicle at the Joginder Nagar guest house as there was no access by road to Barot yet.

Colonel Sir Batty was an elated man. His newfound status as well as the generosity of his seniors towards him pleased him immensely. Three uneventful months passed to the day when he was returning to Joginder Nagar after a visit to Lahore. It was 15 August 1934 and he had been invited to attend a ceremony at the DAV College. After the programme, Sir Humphrey had personally seen him off.

Colonel Sir Batty hummed a tune as his chauffeur drove the car. On entering a hilly terrain of North Punjab, they stopped at the barrier of a level crossing and waited for the train to pass. As it happened at such railroad crossings, one could never guess the length of time required to wait, and so as the minutes ticked by, Colonel Sir Batty began getting fidgety. He did not notice Michael—who over the past three months had become his favourite—look curiously at him through the rear view mirror. Michael's face was expressionless. If only they had crossed over thought Colonel Sir Batty, for the barrier had only just been lowered when they arrived at the railway tracks.

It was a cloudy afternoon and Colonel Sir Batty stepped out of the car and stretched himself. He walked around and stood near a tall tree a few yards before the barricade. He noticed that the small barrier post in that dense forest was being manned by a lone British person, and wondered why the latter would have taken such a job. As though in response, the barrier guard walked over to him smiling and began to explain the reason for his presence in such a remote area. There was no other vehicle or person in sight. It was the cue Michael had been instructed to wait for. He started the engine and, shifting the car into gear, slammed the accelerator down. Without warning and before Colonel Sir Batty could realize what was happening, Michael drove the car into him at full throttle. Colonel Sir Batty was slammed against a tree trunk with a strange and sickening screeching sound. His frail body fell on the ground, crimson blood oozing from where broken ribs had just punctured his sides. The chauffeur's cold, steel-grey eyes were fixed on the spot. Mercilessly, he reversed the car and went crashing one more time into the bleeding man on the ground who gasped for breath, shock on his face. The railway official had stepped aside, as if he knew what was about to happen. The third time, the car crushed Colonel Sir Batty to death. They checked for his pulse. There was no beat. The lifeless, crumpled body was laid on the tracks, and then the men waited till they heard the whistle of the next train—the fast-moving train would do the rest. They went back to Lahore to meet their master, Sir Humphrey, leaving the mutilated body behind.

In the following days, the chauffeur and the British officer in the guise of the guard were duly rewarded for their outstanding contribution in completing the assignment. They, along with the car, were shipped back to London.

When the demise of Colonel Sir Batty was announced and as word of the freak accident spread, people reacted in disbelief. The news sent shock waves throughout North India, particularly in the region of the Punjab. Colonel Sir Batty's death was mourned by thousands of people and many gathered at the cemetery in Lahore for his funeral that was conducted with full state honours.

Articles appeared in newspapers managed by Sir Humphrey stating that the Colonel had wanted to walk across the railroad crossing and had not correctly assessed the speed of the fast-approaching train. Consequently, he had been run over. News also stated that the barrier guard had testified to having witnessed the Colonel being cut to pieces by the train. There was no mention of the chauffeur. Colonel Sir B.C. Batty was laid to rest at a Lahore cemetery. Sir Humphrey was transferred to London and duly awarded for his meritorious service in India. Later, he became advisor to Winston Churchill in the 1940s during World War II. It is another matter that he and Sir Walter Scott were killed when the Luftwaffe bomber planes attacked London on 4 August 1941 and caused devastation there.

Sushil had been speaking continuously for over two hours. He now concluded his narration by saying that Colonel Sir B.C. Batty is still revered and remembered by the villagers even after more than seventy years of the engineer's first arrival in 1912 to the remote area of Barot. And as a mark of respect to the noble soul, every year on 15 August a special ceremony at the government school in the district is held and an award titled 'Colonel Sir B.C. Batty Award for Exemplary Achievement by an Accomplisher is presented to the best student.

For a few minutes we fell silent. The same thought seemed to run in our minds, that what a great man Colonel Sir Batty had been! He had played a pivotal role in changing the course of the history of Barot and North India. No wonder then that he had drawn the kind of respect he had. I broke the silence to thank my brother-in-law for narrating a story that would remain with us forever as a source of inspiration. We spent the next few days enjoying the wonders of Barot, and then we left for Delhi, our hearts filled with a fresh abundance of goodness from the hills.

Today, Barot is rated as one of the most beautiful hill stations of Himachal Pradesh, but for us it will always hold a special place in our hearts for the profound message of courage and foresight it gave us about a colonel who lived his life for others and was a true Accomplisher.

Nightmare in London

It was a cold, crisp winter morning in December. Twenty-two young bikers stood in line at the starting point, ready to be flagged off. The first streaming rays of daylight shone on their gleaming motorbikes as they fixed their eyes on the road ahead. The 120 kilometre stretch of the race, beginning from the periphery of Chandigarh International Airport, would take them through Kalka and Solan upwards into the hills of Shimla, the beauty of Himachal Pradesh.

The latest craze amongst the affluent youth was racing motorbikes with high-speed gears that rushed their adrenalin to a daunting 200 km per hour. That these extraordinary bikes came with high price tags, not to mention the expensive apparel that accompanied them was no constraint. The extremely rich families these young men belonged to could easily afford them this luxury. And so they met regularly every Sunday at the crack of dawn to test the strength of their deadly machines, giving full vent to their passion for the thrilling sport.

Now, as the lads lowered their visors, a gunshot triggered the race. Twenty-two bikes, mostly of Suzuki, Ducati and Triumph, dashed forward...the roar of machines ripping the stillness of the morning air. The bikers staked their claim on the highway and in a bid to outdo each other, plunged the speedometer needle further and further till man and machine were one big mass tearing across the smooth terrain. The winner of the prize money—a neat sum of five lakh rupees, conjointly contributed— was to treat the others to a meal at a luxury hotel in Shimla.

Paramvir was one of the participants of this exclusive group. Son of Manvinder Singh, owner of the Heamstead brand of draught beer manufactured in Punjab, he owned ten racing vehicles that he was extremely proud of. He took special care of his collection of bikes and sports cars that he kept in an exclusive garage at his home in Chandigarh. It was cold on the highway as the race progressed onto the hilly terrain, the temperature hovering at 3 degree Centigrade, but more than the wind-chill, it was the suddenly descending fog that became a cause for concern. Believing, however, that it would lift once the sun shone higher in the sky, the bikers continued. Enthusiastic as they were, they were not going to be deterred so easily. But it led to a disaster—the kind that becomes news in the dailies and sets an example forever.

Near Dharampur, the driver of the Himachal bus service was cautiously taking his sixty-seater vehicle up the hill. As he chugged arduously around a steep bend, he could barely see the road due to the thickened fog. The sight of a vehicle suddenly emerging into view a short distance ahead caught him unawares. He slammed the brakes in the nick of time, managing to avert a collision, but six of the twenty-two bikers close behind at full throttle were not so lucky. As the first one rammed into the bus, it led to a pile-up, and in the ear-splitting crashes that followed, three motorbikes plunged into the gorge below. One of the bikers went down as well while another died on the way to the hospital. Paramvir's was the sixth bike in the collision. He applied his brakes but it was too late to avoid impact. He was severely injured; but luckily, he survived.

∿

The family was seated in the living room. Senior Mr and Mrs Chaddha had summoned the meeting with their daughter Manveen, the oldest of their three children, and son Manvinder, the youngest, at their home in Ambala in Punjab. Manveen had driven down from Amritsar along with her husband Inderjeet, while Manvinder had come from Chandigarh with his wife Harleen and son Paramvir who now, after the accident, was permitted by his doctors to travel. He was still on medication and required another two months of care before he could be declared as fully recovered. Four months had passed since the accident, but for the family it seemed as though an eternity had gone by. To think they had almost lost their one and only grandson gave the senior Chaddhas repeated shocks, and they suffered every time they thought of that morning when they first heard the news of the accident from Manvinder. The family meeting had been called to discuss Paramvir's life and lifestyle. There was tension in the air. The seniors were alarmed at the indulgences Paramvir enjoyed and expressed their indignation. Why was he not doing anything productive after graduating from college? Why did he not join the family business? He was already twenty-four! Racing on a Ducati! How could his parents have allowed him such a dangerous pastime? And so on it went. Awkward and embarrassed, Manvinder and Harleen fidgeted about looking for answers even as Paramvir stared at his parents in complete disbelief; why were they not defending him and why was the situation being made so serious? Yes, the accident had been severe, lives had been lost and he was extremely sorry for what had happened. But one did not stop living or driving. And above all, why call a meeting for it? The parents of the boy knew. They could understand the pain behind the grandparents' anger; only that they had not disclosed it to their son so far.

Matters became worse when Paramvir revealed the reason for his not joining the family business. He wished to go to the UK for higher studies. Manvinder and Harleen looked at the seniors helplessly as the latter stared at Paramvir shell-shocked. They had not been told of this earlier. Paramvir's parents had tried to dissuade him but he would not listen and had asked his parents for an explanation for their refusal. They had given none. Mrs Chaddha began to sob. No one said a word. Then Mr Chaddha, seeming as though to gather courage, spoke firmly to Paramvir telling him he was not to bring up the topic of leaving the country ever again. He was their only grandchild and he was expected to help in the family business. They had given him much to be grateful for, and now it was his duty to respect the wishes of his elders. Paramvir was visibly upset. He argued with his grandfather about how times had changed and how many of his batchmates from college had gone overseas for further studies. But he was silenced by the elders in the room.

Mr Chadha suggested the ultimate cure to Manvinder. He

asked him to get Paramvir engaged to a girl. It would change his ways and get him to take life more seriously. And once he had settled himself in the business, he could be married. Paramvir stormed off in a huff, and even Manvinder's firm calls would not bring him back from the garden where he sat, completely agitated at the interference of his grandparents.

Dinner that evening was a quiet affair. Manveen and Inderjeet played their role as the older couple, making an effort to lighten the air. They brought Paramvir inside and coaxed him to join the rest at the dining table, but no one could eat much. The whole affair had triggered certain thoughts that had upset everyone, and of all of them, Harleen the most. After dinner, Manvinder, Harleen and Paramvir left for Chandigarh. It was the young man who spoke for most of the way, complaining sourly of his grandparents' hold over the family and their unsolicited advice. Manvinder and Harleen remained quiet, and it was only once they had reached home and Paramvir had retired to his room that they dwelt upon the talk of the evening. Maybe they ought to disclose the truth to Paramvir, they discussed. Getting him engaged for marriage was a good idea too. It would certainly have a settling effect on his life. They could make a proposal for Simran, Harleen's best friend's daughter, whom Paramvir was fond of. Having thus mulled over, the couple finally laid their talk to rest. They had decided that Paramvir would be told the next morning and were apprehensive about how he would react. Manvinder went to bed, but Harleen had disturbing thoughts playing on her mind that would not let go of her easily. Making herself some green tea, she sat on the recliner in a corner of the living room and let her mind drift to that part of her that had been alone for many years.

Tears welled up as images began to float in front of her eyes: scenes of the hospital after Paramvir's accident when she first saw him lying there with multiple fractures, the doctor's facial expression when informed her that her son would have to undergo surgeries and not be able to walk for three to four months, the talk of that evening with the parents-in-law... It was this last thought, especially, that triggered much turbulence in her mind. And then she thought of that other hospital...far away...and the endless waiting. In a flash the image of a young, dapper, strikingly handsome man came to her—Paramjit. And in the midst of her tears, she smiled.

Her mind went back to the days when Paramjit had courted her twenty-six years ago. Harleen was all of twenty-one then, and Paramjit was twenty-four. She was extremely charming, and by conventional standards, considered beautiful too. Pammi, as Paramjit was known to his close family and friends, saw her for the first time at The Oberoi Cecil hotel in Shimla during a three-day beauty contest. For the dashing lad, it was love at first sight. For the next two days he kept a watch out for her as she and her friends frequented the hotel to witness the pageant.

It did not take Paramjit long to piece together the information he needed to make his advances towards her. Fortunately, and to his delight, she was from Chandigarh just like him. It would be possible to take his proposed acquaintance with her forward, once they were back in their home city. He must approach her, he thought, for their time in Shimla was short. A little voice urged him on; she was too good to lose! On the last evening of the contest Paramjit met Harleen for the first time. Seated at the table next to hers, he and his friends cheered the contestants on in sync with her group of girls. Fleeting looks and smiles began to pass naturally between the two tables as Paramjit and his friends grabbed every opportunity to speak to them, and in the midst of the programme their tables slowly merged into one large group that cheered excitedly as the winners took their positions on stage. By the end of that evening, he was smiling down into her beautiful eyes and telling her his name. To the pleasantly surprised Harleen, Paramjit asked if she would give him the honour of meeting him the next morning before he left for Chandigarh.

Back in their room that night, the girls spared no chance of teasing Harleen. How lucky she was, they said, and what a handsome guy! Would she meet him? She must!

The two met the next morning at the hotel coffee shop. Phone numbers, addresses and promises were exchanged, and then they parted. Harleen remembered feeling flushed that beautiful morning as she experienced her first butterflies.

They met soon after at the pristine and beautiful Chandigarh Lake. It was to be the first of many a rendezvous. As they walked along the periphery in the cool breeze of the early evening, the two discovered they had much in common. Several such meetings resulted in a closer bond that led eventually to an alliance between them. The families of Harleen and Paramjit came together—they were two well-known and powerful business families of Chandigarh. While Paramjit's father was the owner of one of the first and finest breweries in Punjab, Harleen's father owned a resort near the city. It was a dream wedding. Stretching into a week-long extravaganza, the two families spared no effort in creating the most exotic events over traditional customs and rituals. The interesting spread of delicious cuisines, the unending flow of alcohol, silk and satin, and special flowers imported for the occasion, left guests gasping in admiration. It was a celebration no one could dream of equaling for years to come. The Chaddhas and Cheemas held their status high, and in the midst of the fairytale nuptial, Harleen and Paramjit considered themselves lucky for having been blessed with each other. It was too good to be true.

They had decided on London as their honeymoon destination. They wanted it to be special for it was the start to their new life together as a couple. Harleen remembered it was raining when they landed at Heathrow Airport. Paramjit's cousin Sunny was there to receive them. Not having been able to attend the wedding of his favourite brother who was more like a friend to him, Sunny warmly welcomed the couple, promising them any help that they might require during their stay. They drove to The Savoy hotel. En route to the airport, Sunny had personally seen to the décor of the stylishly-done suite reserved for the newlywed couple, making sure to have the rooms arranged with extra bouquets of flowers. The fragrance and colours of the finest blossoms welcomed the couple as they now walked in.

The next few days, as Harleen recalled, made her best memories. Her Pammi was every bit the devoted and chivalrous husband he had promised to be. It was her first visit to London while he had been there once earlier; so he promised to acquaint her with the best the city had to offer—but only when they could spare the time, he had added laughingly. The first two days went by in a flash. After the mornings spent leisurely lounging around at the hotel, they went out for lunch, followed by hours of touring the city and shopping. Pammi was delighted with her purchases. Her obliging husband ensured she made an exhaustive wishlist of the things she might ever need. He filled her heart with all the love he could give and took extra care that no desire of hers went unfulfilled.

The third day in London was a special one. Sunny had made arrangements for a lavish celebration at The Lloyds Club in Sussex in honour of his cousin and the charming bride. He was an elite member of the prestigious club and had invited his circle of relatives and friends.

As had been decided, Sunny left early for the club to oversee the arrangements. Paramjit, who had invited an old friend of his in London, Dr Ranbir, was to pick him up from St George's Hospital on the way to the club with Harleen. They were to join Sunny by 8.00 p.m.

The couple left The Savoy in a hotel car and arrived at St George's. Paramjit informed his friend over his cell phone and then he went to the reception area to receive him there. Harleen waited in the car. From where it was parked across the road, she had a clear view of the main entrance to the hospital. Her mind began to wander. How fast these events had unfolded, she thought. It was only a year ago, about the same time that she had planned the visit to Shimla to witness the beauty pageant. She sighed happily. It was incredible! At that moment, Harleen could never imagine that events more unbelievable were about to unfold in her life. Expecting her husband to emerge anytime with his friend, she kept her eyes on the entrance, but the time on her watch kept ticking by.

In the reception area as he stood waiting, Paramjit began to feel uneasy. His head spun. Was it fatigue? Had he exhausted himself with all the excitement of the wedding and London? He began to perspire and a severe pain rose in his chest. As he tried to take a step forward, he staggered. The medical staff present there rushed forward to help him. Dr Ranbir, who had just stepped into the waiting area, took one look at his friend and urgently called for a stretcher. He had Paramjit wheeled to the intensive care wing on the sixth floor for immediate medical aid.

All this while Harleen sat in the car, waiting, thinking of the evening ahead and looking forward to having a good time. When half an hour had passed and there was no sign of Paramjit, she began to get anxious. They were getting late. Was the doctor not free yet?

She decided to check for herself. In the waiting area, her husband was nowhere to be seen. Maybe he had gone upstairs to meet Dr Ranbir, she thought, and sat down. There was nothing to do but wait till they showed up. Many minutes passed and then, suddenly, there was a flurry of movement at the entrance. A car screeched to a halt and Harleen saw four or five people clamber out and rush in. The group ran to a side doorway and up the stairs, even as a guard tried to stop them. Her heart sank. She recognized one person—Sunny. What was he doing at the hospital? Who were those people with him? Why were they in a hurry? Harleen began to pray for everything to be fine. But her worst nightmare had just begun.

Her eyes were closed when she felt a hand on her shoulder.

Something was amiss in the expression on Dr Ranbir's face as well as those of Sunny and the others with them. She could sense something terrible had happened. Dr Ranbir and Sunny gently guided her as they led her into an elevator and up to the sixth floor. Harleen always found it difficult to recount the details of what transpired thereafter. She could only remember being in a daze as she was spoken to. The words seemed to come from some deep and dark pit as Dr Ranbir explained what had happened—Paramjit had felt suddenly unwell. They had given him first aid, but his pulse rate dropped and he stopped responding. Two senior heart specialists had tried to save him and given him electric shocks, but they could not revive him. Paramjit faded away, even as the team of medical staff tried desperately to hold on to her husband's life. In minutes it was all over. Paramjit was dead. He had suffered a massive heart attack.

Harleen stared in disbelief. Dead! Nothing made sense. Paramjit gone? Her world collapsed and she started screaming— no, it was not possible. How could he go just like that? It was a mistake, she shouted. She wanted to see Pammi, where was he? But the sight of her husband's body lying on a stretcher, covered and silent, was unbearable for Harleen. The last thing she could remember was lifting the white sheet to look at his face...and then she lost consciousness. Once she came to, Dr Ranbir first checked Harleen before giving her permission to leave. Sunny took her to his home so that his mother could look after her, and she remained there for a couple of days till her family arrived from India. Mr Chaddha and Mr Cheema completed the paperwork required for clearance of the body. Manveen, Paramjit's elder sister, and Mrs Cheema packed her belongings at The Savoy. Harleen did not accompany them; she could not bring herself to face the look of the suite again. Another three days later, the five of them flew back to India with Paramjit's remains. The last rites were performed in Chandigarh.

The days stretched out in front of Harleen...days of complete emptiness. She could not believe at that time that she would ever be herself again. At times she was hysterical and had to be given sedatives. At other times she withdrew into herself and would not speak for days. She stayed at her parents' home. The elders had decided that for the time being it was best for Harleen to stay where she would be more at ease. She needed time to regain her former self, if that were possible, and Paramjit's home was, understandably, unfamiliar to her. After some time had passed they felt the matter of her residence could be discussed. But to everyone's surprise, that happened sooner than expected, for Harleen discovered she was expecting Paramjit's child.

Harleen was distraught. What should have been a time of joy was replaced with immense inner struggle for her. She missed Paramjit more than ever. For the Chaddhas it was a time of reckoning. It was to be the child of the son they had just lost—his light, his memory. Once the baby was born, Harleen must come back, they said.

As the weeks passed, the two families began to have a similar desire—to see her married again. Her parents wished to see her begin life anew; her child would need a father, they thought. Her mother broached the topic once but Harleen would not hear of it. She could not bear to think of another man after Paramjit. Her mother did not insist, and although her heart reached out to her daughter, she refrained from broaching the topic again. Mr and Mrs Chaddha too wanted their daughter-in-law to start her life afresh, but they had another reason for it. They wished that Paramjit's child would grow up in their home.

As Harleen sat on the living room recliner, her thoughts now went to the summer evening when the elders of the two families—the Chaddhas and the Cheemas—met for the discussion that was to change her life. Mr Chaddha began the talk by stating that it was now the responsibility of the elders to settle Harleen's future. Her child should be brought into the world with the name of a living father. Harleen was only twenty-two; it was no age to bring up a child alone. The Cheemas agreed with him. He then suggested that she marry Manvinder, his younger son and Paramjit's younger brother. He could have dropped a bomb for the effect it had.

Manvinder? But that was impossible, said Mr Cheema. Manvinder was only eighteen and had just begun college. It would be unreasonable. How could he propose such a thing? But Mr Chaddha believed it *was* possible. He reasoned that it was an age-old custom in Sikh families such as theirs, as well as in other parts of India wherein, on the death of her husband, a woman was married to the husband's younger brother to provide 'chadar', meaning protection, to her. It was a way to safeguard a family's self-respect. Harleen would live with them and so would the child. The family would remain intact. And since it was a practice in Sikhism that was approved by their Gurus, it would be accepted in society without question. Mr Chaddha suggested they consider it. He would, in the meantime, speak to Manvinder about it, he said.

Harleen protested, it was unthinkable. Manvinder refused the suggestion outright saying they lived in Chandigarh, a modern city. Such obsolete customs shouldn't even be thought about. They would be laughed at. But the two were not given a choice. Eventually, Mr Chaddha's wish prevailed above all else. Soon after, Harleen was married to her brother-in-law in a quiet ceremony and she came to live in Paramjit's home. Two months later, she delivered a baby boy. They called him Paramvir.

Now, as she came back to the present, Harleen blinked hard to stop the tears that fell from her eyes. 'Oh Pammi!' Her heart ached for her first husband. How she wished he were with her at this moment. How she wished he could see his son. She wondered how life would have been if he were still alive. But he was gone! And the years had flown by. Manvinder had tried to be a good husband; he had cared for her, but somewhere a shadow had remained between the two of them. Perhaps it was their memory of Paramjit, as Paramvir had a strong resemblance to his father, or perhaps it was because of their conscious decision never to speak about the past. But Manvinder had been a good father to Paramvir. Harleen respected him for that and also for his decision to never have any children of his own. He did not want that he should ever feel less for Paramvir. Once he was married, Manvinder's carefree days came to an end. After college he joined his father's brewery business. In years to come, they opened another office in Ambala, and senior Mr and Mrs Chaddha shifted base there while Manvinder took charge of the Chandigarh division.

Life had been good for Harleen thereafter and she had no cause for complaint, but now, in the present moment, she wished differently for her son. He must do what made him happy. His life would not be founded on a compromise. Come what may, the mother decided she would stand by her son. She would do it for him even though she could not do much for herself. He stood on the threshold of a new life ahead, he must start with the truth, Harleen believed. As dawn broke in through the curtains of the large windows, she rose with the resolve to see her son through this time that was his. And then she went to bed at peace with herself.

Paramvir did not understand how to react. He looked bewildered. He gaped at his father, or whom he had taken to be his biological father, or rather whose manner towards him he had never questioned, and he did not feel any less for him. For all the love and care he had received throughout his life, it was hard for Paramvir to think how differently he might have felt if his real father were to stand in front of him today. Harleen and Manvinder looked at each other, and what had begun as an apprehensive moment, melted. Father, mother and son reunited as they embraced each other, breaking all barriers between them.

The three sat at the breakfast table talking. There were plans to be made. They would make a proposal to Simran's parents immediately, possibly the same evening, and share with them the details of Paramvir's parentage. It was important that they know before forging an alliance for their daughter. And then there was the other hurdle to be crossed—that of convincing the senior parents about Paramvir's plans of going to the UK for his higher studies. They chuckled as Paramvir mimicked his grandfather's expression on hearing about London. But the three of them were confident they would gain his consent. Now that they had formed a new bond between them, everything would be all right.

⌔

Eight months later, Paramvir left for a postgraduate study programme at King's College London. It was to a packed house in Chandigarh that he bade farewell. The senior Chaddhas had come from Ambala to bless their grandson before his departure and so had his aunt and uncle from Amritsar. Simran's parents were there too. They had willingly consented to their daughter's formal engagement with Paramvir before he left. It was going to be hard being separated from the family, Paramvir thought, and he would miss his fiancée the most. He was thrilled that all had gone well. He thought of his biking days and smiled. Sometimes life's adventures are about charting your life on the path that makes you happy because even that can be a challenge.

When he landed at the airport in London, Paramvir was received by Sunny and the latter's son Amrinder. They were there to receive him and take him on to the next leg of his journey.

Acknowledgments

We would like to thank our parents, Mr. Shanker Kapoor and Mrs Rajni Kapoor who have always been an inspiration to us.

We would also like to thank our respective wives, Punam Kapoor and Manisha Kapoor, for giving us unconditional support and suitable suggestions.

We cannot but thank and acknowledge the contribution by Mrs Anoo Chatrat, a sincere friend and a journalist, for her vital suggestions in giving life to charactors that we had created. We also thank her for spending her valuable time in developing these stories and taking them to a higher pedestal.

Aman, Mahima & Sagarika (Chartered Accountants and Advocates) our children, deserve a special mention here. They managed our professional practice in our absence, allowing us to re-visit places described in these stories.

Lastly we are thankful to the team of Rupa Publications India Pvt. Ltd for agreeing to publish and promote this book under their aegis.